SHATTERED SAINT

BRENTSON UNIVERSITY SERIES
BOOK 4

BRI BLACKWOOD

BRETAGEY PRESS

NOTE FROM THE AUTHOR

Hello!

Thank you for taking the time to read this book. Shattered Saint is a dark college billionaire brother's best friend enemies-to-lovers romance. It is not recommended for minors and contains situations that are dubious and could be triggering. The book also includes underage drinking, binge drinking, stalking, and mentions of a mental disorder which might also be triggering. It isn't a standalone and the book ends in a cliffhanger. The next book in the series is Shattered Sinner.

BLURB

This never should have happened...

He was supposed to be off limits.

After all, my brother's best friend was the one I couldn't have.

There were lines that should never be crossed.

At least until one fateful night

That changed everything forever.

Now we hated each other

And nothing was going to change that.

Ever.

Or so I thought...

PLAYLIST

In My Blood — Shawn Mendes
LoveGame — Lady Gaga
no tears left to cry — Ariana Grande
Flame — Tinashe
I'm A Mess — Bebe Rexha
Shameless — Camila Cabello
Jaded — Miley Cyrus
The Heart Wants What It Wants — Selena Gomez
Water Under The Bridge — Adele
I Don't Wanna Live Forever — ZAYN, Taylor Swift

The playlist can be found on Spotify.

1

BIANCA

A LITTLE MORE THAN TWO YEARS AGO

The warm summer breeze that drifted into my room should have left me feeling relaxed. Instead, I was staring down at the half-empty bottle of vodka contemplating if I was going to drink from it. Everything in me screamed not to do what I was thinking about doing, but the will to stop was nowhere to be found.

Anxiety and panic were closing in on me. I knew it was only a matter of time before I succumbed to it and ended up curled into a ball on my bathroom floor, wishing that I would die right where I laid. I needed an escape, even temporarily, from the pain I was feeling.

I walked out onto my balcony and stood there for a moment. With the number of cars that were parked outside my home, I could only imagine how many people were downstairs.

My fingers trembled as I adjusted my hold on the bottle. Deep down, I knew I was being foolish for doing this, but that had never stopped me before. Without another thought, I uncapped the bottle and brought it to my lips. I could feel the tears sitting in the corners of my eyes. In one swift motion, I downed some of the liquid. I couldn't deny that I enjoyed the warming sensation following the liquor as it traveled down my throat.

As the alcohol moved through my body, I closed my eyes, tears threatening to fall. The light breeze was a strong contrast to the heat that filled my body. Alcohol was excellent at numbing the pain, but I knew it wasn't something I should rely on. Yet I still did.

With a heavy sigh, I walked back into my bedroom, shutting the glass doors behind me. I put the vodka back in its hiding place and took a breath mint in an effort to mask the smell of what I'd done.

I jumped when a loud thud brought my attention to the door. It was a sound I'd been anticipating yet it still felt as if it had come too soon.

Shit.

It was time.

My attempt at procrastination was over.

While I wanted to stay in my safe haven, that knock on the door was the sign that my solitude was about to come to an end. My pulse quickened as I inched closer to the door. I should have been prepared for what was about to come, but I wasn't. Now, there was no turning back.

Being alone was usually a source of comfort for me and before right now, it had been hours since I'd been alone. My mother hired a team to turn me into the belle of the ball and after they left, it was just me and the silence that I both loved and feared.

My fear was due to being left with my thoughts, and the

anticipation of what was to come tonight had nearly made me throw up.

As I caught a glimpse of myself in the mirror near my door, I couldn't help but think that at least my mother couldn't complain about my appearance tonight. My blonde hair was down in loose curls, falling along my bare shoulders. My tea length cocktail dress was navy blue and I paired it with nude-colored pumps. I had been made into the perfect image of the mirage I was supposed to uphold tonight. All that mattered was that my parents were pleased with how I looked, and now it was time for me to leave.

As my fingers touched the doorknob, my body trembled slightly. My grasp on the metal made me realize how nervous I really was. My hand's clamminess made the coldness of the knob more shocking and forced goose bumps to appear on my arms.

I hated that I'd been forced into this, but there was no way I was admitting that out loud. Not that anyone would listen to me anyway.

Thankfully, I wasn't going into this situation completely blind. I had an idea of what to expect. Yet I still felt as if I was being thrown to the wolves.

Questions about whether this would be worth it in the end circled my brain, but there wasn't much I could do about it now. I had to open the door and step through it, no matter what the consequences.

I steeled myself and twisted the doorknob, opening it up to a world where money ruled everything. I found my mother standing on the other side of the door.

I watched as her heavily made-up face looked over me, probably impressed with the work her beauty team had been able to perform. When she finally met my eyes, a look of disappointment crossed her face.

She stared at me for a moment, but didn't say a word. I waited for her to mention that she smelled alcohol, but she didn't. If I had to guess, between the mint and how distracted she was by everything else, me drinking something hadn't crossed her mind.

"Bianca, it's about time you came out of there. We need to get downstairs before your father notices that neither of us are there."

I was certain the chances of my father realizing I wasn't there were low. I struggled to hold my tongue. The right thing to do would have been to just agree and then make my way downstairs, but for some reason, I couldn't.

"He'll be okay. It's not like he's going to pass out and fucking die."

"Bianca, watch your mouth. Just because you're legally an adult, doesn't mean I'll tolerate that type of language in my house. Especially tonight."

I rolled my eyes and debated saying the insult on the tip of my tongue. Was it really worth the fight tonight? Probably not, but I had a hard time backing down from anything.

With a heavy sigh, I bit my tongue. This time, I would be the bigger person, but I wouldn't make any promises that this would always be the case.

"Fine. Let's go then."

My mother seemed pleased with my response even though there wasn't a hint of joy in my words. I joined her in the hallway and together we walked toward what would be one of the most challenging days of my life.

At first, the only thing that could be heard was the

clicking of our heels along the marble floor, but the closer we got to our destination, the more sounds I heard. The clinking of glasses and soft murmurs could be heard as we walked toward the stairs.

In just a few moments, I would be paraded in front of a bunch of rich people as Van Henson's daughter. It would be quite the spectacle because my father was mayor of Brentson, and he was also one of the richest men in all of New York.

That came with a price on multiple fronts.

My father was ambitious. He wanted more power and more money. He had higher aspirations than just being mayor of our town, and there was nothing better than growing his wealth. My mother was pretty much along for the ride and would do what she could to help him achieve his dreams.

Hence why I was all dressed up tonight and walking down our grand staircase to the party below. When we reached the bottom, the first thing that greeted me was the smell of delicious food being prepared. Of course, my parents had pulled out all the stops to treat their guests as if they were royalty. What made this comical was that I was willing to bet my parents couldn't give two shits about most of the people in attendance tonight. My parents were fantastic at putting on a façade and more often than not, talked trash about most of their guests. To be honest, I would be surprised if the feeling wasn't mutual.

But our true feelings didn't matter. Tonight was meant to go perfectly. After all, we were the picture-perfect family that everyone strived to be.

My mother tapped me on the back, a small warning to me to straighten my posture because we'd reached the main floor, arriving at our stage for the night. We needed to have our masks on because any hint of a scandal could set off my father's friends, adversaries, and everyone in between.

Most people thought that New York City's elite were vicious, and that was true. Many of Brentson's citizens had moved here from New York City, meaning those attitudes carried over here sometimes.

How did I know this?

Because I had to drift between these different sectors, and it made things... interesting, to say the least. Not to mention the political landscape we also needed to navigate, and the procedures we needed to follow because of my father's job and to prevent any hint of scandal. A misstep in that arena could lead to dire consequences that I would never hear the end of.

I'd mostly been kept out of this circus because of my age. I will say my parents did allow me to have something that resembled a normal childhood, and I was grateful for that. Now that I was seventeen, I felt as if I was being thrown head-first into the lion's den with no way to survive.

There's a common belief that your parents are supposed to protect you as much as possible from the evils of this world. But my parents? They had no problem with making deals with the devil.

Deals. As in multiple.

Another reason why my parents wouldn't be winning any parents of the year awards any time soon was because they decided to throw this party today. This should have been an important day for our family being that it was only hours after my older brother's high school graduation. I knew without a doubt, he would have wanted to hang out with his girlfriend and his friends. He should have been celebrating his success instead of being at this stuffy ass party for my parents.

Although I hoped that Nash and my parents didn't get into it tonight, I wouldn't blame him if they did. Speaking of, where was Nash anyway?

I looked around as much as my body would allow me without alerting my mother, but my brother wasn't anywhere to be found.

The last time I saw him was about an hour after we arrived home from his graduation ceremony. If he didn't show up tonight, that would be a big fuck you to my parents, and I would be thrilled.

It was harsh, but that was life.

"Bianca."

I ignored my mother and eyed a server as they walked by with a tray full of hors d'oeuvres, and the quick whiff of its aroma was lovely. My stomach growled in response, and it was then I realized I hadn't eaten in hours.

"Would you like one, miss?"

I nodded and grabbed a bacon-wrapped date and a napkin. I gave a small grin before popping the food into my mouth. As I was chewing, I turned to look at my mother.

She made a show of brushing off my dress as if a mysterious wrinkle had managed to appear on the bodice. I knew there was none, and her actions might have been the result of her being nervous.

My mother snatched the napkin out of my hand and whipped it at my face, to get rid of any crumbs I assumed. "Remember to be polite and to smile often. This is something you hate, but you can relax when everyone is gone."

I wanted to slap her hands away from me, but that would go against everything I was supposed to portray tonight. Keeping my cool tonight might mean that my mother and father had won this battle, but I could still use this to my advantage. There would be many options at my disposal, and I wanted to keep all of them open.

I took a couple of steps before I found myself frozen in place. The foyer of our home led into the ballroom where our guests were gathered. My heart landed at my toes. The anxiety that I felt in my room returned tenfold. I tried to calm my breathing as the feeling of the walls closing in on me tried to knock me down to the point where I might not be able to function. My focus was on making sure I survived this night without having a full-blown panic attack.

My mother's voice cut through my thoughts. "Are you ready?" Impatience dripped off her every word, and I wasn't surprised.

It took everything within me to not yell the word no and run in the opposite direction, but I didn't. Instead, I was forced to deal with a light chill that I wasn't sure if I should attribute to the temperature in the room or the iciness from Mom.

"Yes, *Mother*." I only called her by the term when I was especially irritated with something she'd done. This was definitely one of those times.

I let my mother lead the way into the ballroom and the first thing that caught my eye was how the room had been transformed to fit tonight's festivities. A string quartet sat in one of the corners of the room, playing soft music and creating a calm ambiance for a crowd that was anything but. Several round tables covered in white silk tablecloths displayed centerpieces that included flowers and small candles. The floral scent was pleasant and not overpowering. I was beginning to wonder if my mother was treating this event as a second coming of her wedding, since my father tended to defer to her or his team when it came to décor choices for the events they hosted.

The extensive bar at the other end of the room drew my attention. It would take some effort to get over there, but it would be well worth it, and it would make tonight more bearable. That would be the only way I would be able to deal with this, so I suspected others felt the same. There was no doubt in my mind that the bar had been stocked with the best liquor and wine because my parents loved to pull out all the stops.

I looked up and saw the chandelier that was the centerpiece of the room. It was something that took my breath away every time I entered. However, this time something else was responsible for my sudden inability to breathe.

The number of people that my parents invited tonight was more than I was expecting. The room was filled with the people I expected: CEOs of companies, politicians, celebrities, socialites, and several people who probably wanted to be in one of these groups. I was surprised that members of the media hadn't figured out a way to sneak in here as well. Then again, maybe they had.

The guests mingled with one another effortlessly, with their champagne flutes clutched in their manicured hands. Laughter floated through the air, mingling with the soft strains of classical music playing in the background. The shift in the air as people noticed my mother and me was obvious. I had the distinct feeling that everyone was staring at us rather than talking to each other.

I hated this, but I needed to suck it up and get it over with. The countdown to when I could go back to my room was officially on.

I watched as my mother changed into politician's wife mode before she leaned over and whispered, "I'm going to find your father."

I quickly debated whether I wanted to beg her to stay with me and deal with her company, or if it was worth facing the wolves alone. She didn't leave me much room to convince her otherwise because she was gone before I could say a word.

Out of the corner of my eye, I saw someone begin to walk by me, and when I turned to see who it was, I gave myself a pat on the back because my manifesting powers had worked. Before I could think about it for a second longer, I instinctively reacted. I grabbed a glass of white wine with the confidence of someone who had done it time and time again.

And I had, even though I was underage.

I checked to see if my parents were looking at me, but unsurprisingly, they were both engrossed in the conversations they were having. Not that I was completely sure what they would do if they'd caught me in the act. Sure, it was improper given the time and place, but causing a scene wasn't what they would want to do either. I hesitated for a second before lifting the glass to my lips.

The drink was refreshing and just what I needed to get through the night. Hopefully, it would help me mask my anger and annoyance at having to deal with this.

At least I didn't have this to complain about.

I heard someone clear their throat near me, taking my attention away from my wine. I looked over and found what looked to be a couple standing near me. Given how close they were, how hadn't I noticed them before? Was the wine hitting me hard already? I was sure the swig of vodka I had earlier in the night wasn't helping.

"Isn't this party wonderful?" she gushed to her date. "I simply have to find out who catered the event."

The man she was talking to remained non-expressive, but that was okay because I'd had enough feelings about what she'd just said for the both of us. I cringed internally and took another sip of my wine. It might be me being egotistical, but I was willing to bet that she'd said that for my benefit. When she glanced at me, she confirmed my suspicions.

Although I wanted to do something else, I hid what I truly felt by forcing myself to smile at the woman and her date. The last thing I wanted to hear was that I was rude because I'd side-eyed someone.

"There you are."

It was a voice I recognized immediately, but his sudden appearance behind me almost made me jump out of my skin. I glanced over my shoulder and my brother came into view. Of course, he would show up when I had a drink in my hand, and I wasn't looking forward to the shit he was going to give me because of it.

"What do you mean 'there you are?'" I asked. "I've been here for several minutes, and this is only the first time I'm seeing you."

"I was with Dad, who has been trying to introduce me to what feels like everyone in the room. He dropped your name a few times to some of the men here as well."

Dad mentioning me to some of his associates was weird, but I didn't react to Nash's news. "That's funny, because it seemed as if Mom had no problem leaving me here to fend for myself."

"I'm surprised she left you. Normally she'd be afraid to in case you did something she didn't approve of."

I had to admit, I was surprised too. "She went to look for Dad, so I assume that was more important in her eyes."

Nash shrugged, but didn't offer anything else to that part of our conversation.

"You know you shouldn't be drinking alcohol."

I rolled my eyes. I expected him to say that at some point, but for some reason, it had left my mind just as quickly as it entered it after I saw him. "Who's going to stop me?"

Should I be challenging my brother about this right now? Probably not, but at times I reverted back to when we were younger, and he was bossing me around because he was about a year older.

"Not me, as long as you do one thing for me."

I raised an eyebrow at him. "What are you going to do?"

"Leave as soon as I get the chance. I might need you to cover for me if Mom or Dad asks you anything."

That was easy enough. "That's worth a bit more than you just keeping quiet about me drinking. You're going to owe me for that."

"Fine."

I was surprised. He'd agreed more quickly than I was expecting, making me suspicious. "Where are you going?"

"You don't need to know that."

"So, you're going to see Raven. Got it."

Nash's silence told me all I needed to know. I wasn't

surprised he was going to see his girlfriend of two years this evening, and I didn't blame him one bit. Especially after all this.

I watched my brother as I took another sip of my wine, making sure to stare him down as I did so. When I was done drinking, I flipped my blonde hair over my shoulder and my eyes migrated to the entrance of the ballroom as a way to manifest my ability to exit.

The next thing I saw was *him*.

2

BIANCA

"Look who's here," my father announced to my brother and me.

My eyes widened as I turned to him, partially surprised that he had snuck up on me also. Who was he talking about? I followed the direction of his gaze and saw it was trained on the dude I'd been watching.

If I had to guess, the guy who'd drawn both my attention and my father's had to be around my age or slightly older. Two people, a man and a woman, were standing next to him. The resemblance was strong enough between the cute guy and the older man that I assumed they were his parents. Since my father was jazzed about their arrival, this family more than likely had wealth or power. For some reason, I was leaning toward both.

Normally, I wouldn't be the slightest bit interested in anything related to people my father associated with, but my gaze remained fixated on the younger guy.

His dark brown hair was slightly curly and grazed the collar of his shirt. Maybe it was just my imagination, but it looked as if he'd been running his fingers through it just before he stepped into my house. It gave him a slightly rebellious edge even though he was in a black suit and tie. His shoulders and broad chest filled out the suit perfectly, as if it was custom made for him, and I wouldn't be surprised if it was.

I couldn't tell the exact shade of his eyes from where I was standing, but they looked to be on the lighter end, potentially blue or green. I watched as his eyes scanned the room until his gaze landed on me. It could have been my anxiety talking, but staring at him was intimidating, yet I couldn't look away. His stare was intoxicating, making it difficult to look elsewhere.

Based on how he presented himself, I could tell that his confidence was through the roof, and if I looked like him, I suspected mine would be too. His chiseled jaw was something you would expect to see on a famous actor in a blockbuster movie. When my gaze landed on his lips, they turned into a half-smile, as if he was able to read my mind.

Everything about this guy screamed fuckboy, but that didn't deter me one bit.

When the woman, who I assumed was his mother, leaned over to talk to him, he broke the stare down we were having, and the pressure that I'd felt under his gaze lifted. It was as if I could breathe freely again even with me still being held under the constraints of having to be at this event.

I slowly put my drink down on a high table to my left and as I stood straight up again, my father put his hand on my back and pushed me forward. I glared at him, but of course he didn't notice because all his attention was drawn to the people who had just walked into our home.

"Oliver Beaumont! It's so great of you and your family to join us," my father said as he walked over to new arrivals. My mother and Nash followed behind him as I tried not to show what I was really feeling.

Having been raised by the man, it was obvious to me when he'd put on his political voice. The smooth, authoritative tone that he had been practicing and perfecting for as long as I could remember was easy to spot. The two men shook hands as the rest of us stood back, awkwardly waiting for our introductions.

Following his lead, I forced my shoulders back and gave an award-winning smile. It was fake as hell, but my parents couldn't say I didn't put in any effort. The guy who'd caught my attention the moment he'd walked into the room was watching me, seeming somewhat amused by my acting job.

"Thank you for inviting us. You have a beautiful home," Mr. Beaumont said.

Our fathers shook hands and then my father turned to give the rest of us room to be introduced. From where I was standing, it looked as if both men gave each other a firm handshake, making sure not to show any signs of weakness or intimidation.

Dad gestured to each one of us as he said, "This is my wife, Elizabeth, and my children, Nash and Bianca." He then turned back to the Beaumont family and said, "This is Oliver, Amelia, and Easton."

Easton. His name was Easton. I didn't know what I was expecting it to be, but it wasn't that.

"It's nice to meet you," my mother's voice cut through the chatter in my brain, and she followed my dad's lead by shaking each member of the Beaumont family's hand.

Nash and I followed suit, and the last people to shake hands were Easton and me.

Being this close to him was setting my brain on fire and caused something else. I couldn't quite describe it because of the storm of emotions that were crashing through me in his presence. If I hadn't known any better, I would have thought that my heart was about to burst out of my chest, given how hard it was beating.

It could have been the way that his eyes, which I could now confirm were a beautiful green, followed my every move. It was unsettling, but something I couldn't back away from. On the surface he was calm, but there was something behind his eyes that I couldn't quite place, and I was intrigued.

Or was I making it up?

All of this was before our hands touched.

When they did, I startled with a small, involuntary jump, and a slight smile from Easton confirmed he noticed the effect he was having on me. While I'd had crushes in school, I'd never been so taken aback by someone I barely knew.

We shook hands for several seconds longer than necessary, and when he finally let my hand go, I could still feel the tingle from his touch.

"Nash and Easton have already been talking to one another."

Those words drew my attention away from Easton and back to my father who'd spoken them.

"What are you talking about, Van?"

"Since Easton and Nash are going to Brentson University in the fall, where they'll both be playing football, we sent the boys each other's numbers a few weeks ago," my father said to everyone. "Tonight was just a great time for all of us to meet in person, however."

Shit. Nash hadn't mentioned anything about Easton, not that he usually told me anything about his friends anyway. I'd already had red flags about Easton because we'd been introduced by my father. My father's attempts to make sure that Easton was going to be friendly with my brother further complicated things.

Why was I thinking this anyway? I barely knew this guy, but my brain was still going haywire. Could it be because of my lack of a dating life?

Being the mayor's daughter made dating dull to say the least. I still had one more year of high school to go, and while I'd gone on a few dates here and there, nothing was serious. I hadn't met the love of my life in high school, unlike my older brother. Maybe it was my paranoia speaking, but high school was... well high school. While I would argue that my experience was pretty good, knowing who to trust was an entirely different thing.

Given my father's position in this town, it further ensured that I didn't trust many people. So, while many of my classmates were out partying at each other's homes when their parents weren't there, I mostly kept to myself; the lonely virgin who lived in the big house just outside of the town's center.

"Bianca, Nash, your mother and I need to go and speak to our guests, and I want to introduce Mr. and Mrs. Beaumont to a few people. Will you three be okay?"

My father wasn't actually concerned about our well-being, he was only making sure we didn't do anything that would embarrass him. Luckily, I didn't have to answer him because Nash answered for all of us.

"We'll be fine," Nash responded.

I watched as our parents made their way to the crowd, leaving Nash, Easton, and me by ourselves.

"Are parties at your house always like this?"

I turned to look at Easton and it was the first time I'd heard him speak. His voice was a bit deeper than I was expecting and I hated that it immediately drew me in. Between his words and the look in his eyes, his playfulness took me by surprise. I didn't think he was saying what he said to be a dick, but more so because he wanted to break the ice that had frozen over us the moment our parents had left.

"This type of thing? Pretty much. It's what my parents prefer. This is kind of like their safety net; if you will," Nash offered.

"I hate this shit."

Both Nash and Easton's heads swung toward me, and I shrugged. The alcohol was making me feel more brazen than normal, but they were both just going to have to deal with it.

"Don't look at me like that, Nash. We both know you agree with me. What would you give to not have to do all of this?" I shouldn't have been sharing my thoughts in front of a stranger like this, but I didn't care. I'd blame that on the alcohol in the morning.

Nash glanced at Easton and then looked ahead. He didn't give me a response, but that answered my question anyway. He caught the eye of a waiter who was carrying a tray with glasses of water on it.

"Do either of you want anything to drink? Some of us could use this water more than others."

I rolled my eyes even though he was right. Nash did the honors of handing us each a cup, and I made a show of taking a dramatic sip from mine. The water was refreshing, and if I couldn't finish that wine I grabbed, it was the next best thing.

Was I being immature about all of this? Yes, but I still did it.

"What I really need is a cup of coffee with cream and two sugars," I mumbled to myself.

"Being the children of the town's mayor sounds like an amazing experience."

My attention was brought back to Easton, who I almost forgot was standing there due to my irritation with Nash. My lips twitched in response to his comment. His sarcasm was more than welcomed. He raised his glass as if to toast us and brought it to his lips. Was it weird to be fascinated by the way he drank his water?

Fuck, I needed to get out more.

Since he'd already witnessed some of our drama, I felt somewhat comfortable letting him in on a little more. "Sometimes the level of scrutiny we are under is a lot. Well, our father's political career is a lot."

I had mixed feelings about complaining about the privilege I had, but talking to Nash and Easton felt as if I was turning a corner. I usually kept my feelings close to the chest, only confiding in my best friend, Iris, about them but the pressure on me tonight wasn't helping.

I turned away from Nash and Easton briefly when the chattering from the guests in my house grew louder. I saw my parents standing in a sea of people, talking, and I suspected that was the reason for the increase in volume. It was easy to see that they were living their best lives while I felt the exact opposite. At least I had a handsome guy in front of me to keep me distracted.

"While I haven't had the same experience, I can understand what it could be like. I'm not a fan of these types of things either, but I made a deal with my parents to show up here tonight. Now I'm not regretting that decision."

Once again, Easton's words snapped me back to the conversation in front of me. Was he flirting with me? I was slightly impressed that he was doing it with my brother standing right here. When I turned around to face them again, Easton was looking at me once more. The look in his eyes told me that there should be no question in my mind about his intentions.

"No regrets, huh?" I needed to tread somewhat carefully because I didn't want to make things awkward with Nash here. "That's good, but what will they be giving you in exchange for this?"

"I haven't decided yet. Sometimes, I save my favors up for the right occasion."

His words shouldn't have had an effect on me, but the intensity from his gaze forced me to stop thinking for a second. I wondered if there was a double meaning behind his words and if they were referring to the gravitational pull between the two of us.

Nash let out a loud cough, stopping the moment Easton and I were having dead in its tracks. Then he said, "Mom and Dad are about to speak."

I turned and watched as my father helped my mother up onto the makeshift stage that had been created for them so that they could be the center of attention. I couldn't deny that my parents knew how to present the picture-perfect marriage on the surface. They were in sync with one another. Every move they made dripped with elegance, and their admiration for each other was evident. At least in public that appeared to be the case.

After her introduction by the emcee for the night, my mother adjusted the microphone at the clear podium and gave a warm smile. "Good evening and welcome to our home. I want to thank each and every one of you for coming here this evening."

As her remarks continued, I noticed that, in the process of the crowd gathering around the stage, Easton had positioned himself between Nash and me. He was standing close enough that I could swear I felt the warmth from his body. When his hand brushed against me, it set my skin on fire. I let my mind temporarily wander to what could be if he'd touched me with the intention of ruining me for anyone else.

I did my best to bring my attention back to my mother, and I was delighted to hear that she was wrapping up her speech.

"And now, I'm so happy to have the honor to introduce our mayor and my husband, Van Henson."

The applause was thunderous. If it hadn't been, I knew my father would have made a point of complaining about it later. My parents hugged one another before my mother stepped aside and let my father take his place behind the podium. His practiced smile was firmly in place, and he gave a small wave as the volume from everyone's cheers began to die down in anticipation of his remarks.

"Thank you, thank you," my father said as he scanned the crowd and bought some time before he launched into his speech for the night. "Thank you so much for coming to our home tonight. I'm so happy to be here with my beautiful wife, Elizabeth, and my lovely children, Nash and Bianca."

The applause picked up again and Nash gave a small wave, acknowledging it. I followed suit as Dad looked in the crowd and waved back at us. The guests standing near us cheered, and Easton joined in by clapping too. It took a moment before the crowd turned back to the main attraction.

My father waited a beat before he spoke again. "Family is the reason why I do this. Without them, I wouldn't be standing here in front of you. Without their support, none of this would exist."

I sighed loudly enough that it drew Easton's gaze. Out of the corner of my eye, I saw him look over at me, but I ignored him. I didn't want to draw attention to the fact that I thought what my father was saying was bullshit. The way that Dad was able to speak with such conviction made me wish what he was saying was true instead of a bunch of lies. I hated that I longed for the man he presented to the world, instead of the one he only showed in private.

I did my best to focus on what he was saying in case someone was watching me to get my reaction. Anything to avoid being talked about was usually on the top of the list. I listened to my father's rehearsed lines and began saying the speech along with him in my head. I'd heard it enough times given how much he'd practiced it, sometimes using my mom, Nash, and me as his audience.

"Let's raise a toast," my father concluded, "to family and a beautiful, positive future for Brentson!"

The guests followed my father's lead and raised their glasses too. I turned to look at Nash, who'd also raised his water, and then my gaze moved to Easton. Everyone else faded into the background as my eyes connected with his. We exchanged a small nod, as if we were having our own private toast, and I brought my cup to my lips. I was back to wanting alcohol, but this water would have to do. We took a sip together, and I couldn't help but bask in this appearing to be our own private moment in this sea of people. Was this real or was I making it into something that it wasn't?

I broke our connection by turning toward my brother and I asked, "Do you mind holding this while I go to the bathroom?"

"Sure."

I handed the water off and walked away from Nash and Easton. I got stopped by a few people on my way, but at least it happened before I went into the bathroom. When I exited, no one stopped me on the way back to Nash and Easton, but it was obvious to me that something had changed while I was gone.

When I was a few feet from them, based on the way both their arms were crossed, it looked as if they were having a tense conversation. Nash looked over at me, forcing their discussion to come to a halt.

"I'm sure Mom and Dad will be over here soon, so I'm going to head out. If they ask where I am..."

"I'll tell them that I have no idea," I said.

"Excellent. I'll see you later." Nash cut his eyes over at Easton before he gave me a small nod and walked away, choosing to head toward the back of our house versus leaving through the front door.

It was then that it hit me that I was alone with Easton, but that didn't last for long.

"Bianca! Bianca!" my mother exclaimed as she walked toward me. "I have some people I want you to meet."

Of course she did. I looked at Easton and said, "I'll see you later?"

"Sure," Easton replied. The finality in his voice made me wonder if he was telling the truth.

My mother looked between Easton and me before she said, "Your parents should be making their way over here right now. I'm sorry to take her away."

My eyes widened, but before I could say something, my mom grabbed my arm and pulled me away, leaving me wishing I could be with Easton for the rest of the night.

3

EASTON

The last thing I wanted to do was be at this party tonight. There were a million things I could be doing, but attending an event at a politician's house wasn't one of them.

It had taken a lot of bribing on my parents' end to get me to come here tonight. It had gotten to the point where they were almost begging. They didn't give me any insight as to why they were so desperate for me to come, but I couldn't wait to cash in on the favor that they now owed me.

What I also didn't know was why they were attending this party in the first place.

We were new to Brentson. Heck, we hadn't even officially moved into town yet. My parents had just bought a house here because I would be attending Brentson University in just a few short months. It wasn't much of a shift for me since my acceptance and enrollment into the university had been a done deal months before I graduated from high school, but Mom had decided that she wanted a place where they could come and stay. What made it nicer was that it was only a couple of hours outside of New York City so they wouldn't be too far from the city but could escape from it when they wanted.

Brentson seemed like the perfect place for them to get some peace and quiet away from the busy life they tended to lead. Next would be furnishing their new home and figuring out where I would be staying during my time here because I had no intention of living with them.

While my parents were in the process of finding their newest home, they'd been introduced to Mayor Van Henson through family friends. After a discussion with him, they'd gotten an invitation to this party tonight. When Dad told me this whole story, I hadn't been expecting them to accept the invitation, but here we were.

If I had to guess, I would say that my family was one of the few in this room who hadn't donated to Van Henson's campaign. I was sure his mission was to change that as quickly as possible. Having someone kiss your ass in hopes for money being exchanged wasn't high on my list of things I wanted to deal with even if his main focus was on my parents' wallets.

However, there was one redeeming factor about my being here tonight.

Bianca.

She'd taken my breath away the moment I saw her, and I could tell that she was into me too. It made wearing this stuffy-ass suit worth it. Talking to her, even with her older brother standing nearby, was the highlight of this evening by a long shot.

Now I had to watch her walk away. Granted, she was only going to the bathroom and would be back in a few minutes, but still, I was mentally counting down the seconds until she returned, even when I shouldn't.

"Easton," Nash's voice broke through my thoughts, and while I was slightly irritated by the intrusion, I wasn't surprised by it. It would have been awkward for us to be standing here in silence while we waited for Bianca to return. I watched as he crossed his arms over his chest and the friendly expression that had been on his face only moments before was gone. "We need to talk."

Him getting right to the point wasn't a shock to me either. The few text messages that we exchanged because our fathers wanted us to do so had made that clear. Most people in general, but especially at events like this, loved small talk, so having someone in my presence that wasn't about to talk in circles around what he really wanted to say was more than appreciated.

It was obvious to me that he was trying to be intimidating, but I was more amused than anything. I adjusted my stance to mirror his and said, "Go on."

Before he said another word, Nash glanced in the direction that Bianca had walked in and if I hadn't known what he wanted to talk to me about before, I definitely knew now.

"I don't know you well—"

I cut him off before he could continue. "You don't know me at all."

When I spoke, Nash's eyes shot back to me. The tension between the two of us increased tenfold. If looks could kill, I knew he would have taken the opportunity to do so. Interrupting him did little to help with the situation at hand, but I still did it. It was also my way of letting him know that he, too, should tread lightly.

"Whatever thoughts you're having about my sister? Erase them because nothing is going to happen there. Ever."

A multitude of thoughts collided in my mind, and I couldn't believe he had the audacity to say this. I'd done nothing that would allude to my intentions regarding Bianca outside of being friendly. His accusations did little to simmer the irritation I was experiencing.

"I have no idea what you're talking about." That was a lie. I knew what he was referring to.

"I can see the way you're looking at her. I know what's going through your head."

"Once again, you don't know me at all. Your sister should be given the opportunity to make her own decisions."

Nash's jaw clenched and his shoulders stiffened. I knew if we hadn't been at this event right now, he would have thrown a punch. Then again, based on how he was looking at me and clearly struggling to keep his emotions in check, he still might.

"I know she can, but I'm taking care of this little problem for her. So once again, let me make myself perfectly clear. Stay away from Bianca."

"There's nothing little about me, Nash." I let my comment sit in the air and marinate between the two of us. I watched as his eyes flashed and I knew he was going to hit me, but to save him the embarrassment, I said, "I wasn't thinking about her in that way, but don't try to tell me what to do. Trust me, the ending won't be pretty."

"Let's keep it that way. When it comes to my sister, I'll do anything to protect her. Remember that." Nash paused for a moment before unfolding his arms and sticking his hand out in front of him. "If you promise not to go anywhere near her, I'll forget that we ever had this conversation."

I stared at his hand, unsure of how this was going to play out. With my arrival in Brentson, I'd entered his playground. Since I was the new kid in town and plenty of people from all over the world came to Brentson just to go to school, pissing Nash Henson off right out the gate wouldn't be the best decision I'd ever made. Especially because of the relationship that was now developing between our parents.

I wasn't exactly sure about the pros and cons of my parents' newfound "friendship" with the Hensons, but I knew that there was a reason for my parents showing up tonight and it wasn't just to socialize. There was more than likely a lot riding on this, and I couldn't throw it all away over thinking Bianca Henson was hot as fuck.

"Easton?" Nash's face hardened as his patience with me waned.

I waited another couple of seconds before I extended my hand and together, we shook on it. "You have a deal."

Nash smiled at me, happy that we came to a decision that was beneficial for him. The uneasy feeling that crept up my spine about us talking about this behind Bianca's back had only grown stronger.

"Good."

The heavy air that surrounded us lifted, but that didn't lessen my annoyance about this situation. I folded my arms across my chest again and this time, Nash mirrored me. Out of the corner of my eye, I saw Bianca was walking toward us, having no idea what had just occurred between her brother and me.

Nash turned to his sister and said, "I'm sure Mom and

Dad will be over here soon, so I'm going to head out. If they ask where I am..."

"I'll tell them that I have no idea," she replied.

"Excellent. I'll see you later." Nash cut his eyes over at me before he gave Bianca a small nod. He walked away and I was alone with Bianca.

It didn't escape me that he'd now left me alone with her after this deal he came up with. Was this a test? The tension in my arms was becoming unbearable as I resisted the urge to pull her into my embrace and take her out of this room that she clearly wanted to leave. What the hell was wrong with me?

"Bianca! Bianca!" I looked over my shoulder and watched as Elizabeth, Nash and Bianca's mother, walked toward us. "I have some people I want you to meet."

Bianca turned to me, and I stood there, momentarily stunned. I debated coming up with an excuse for why she should stay here, but I thought better of coming between her and her family.

"I'll see you later?" Her voice showcased her vulnerability, and I could only imagine what was going through her mind.

"Sure," I said in return.

Her mother looked between Bianca and I, and then she said, "Your parents should be making their way over here right now. I'm sorry to take her away."

Before another word could be spoken, Bianca's mother grabbed her arm and pulled her away. It was probably for the best.

I found myself debating what I wanted to do as I awkwardly stood around. I didn't want to get pulled into another conversation with someone I didn't know. I looked around the room to see if I could spot my parents but came up short. Before someone could take this as an opportunity to take pity on me and start up a conversation, I left the ballroom and walked into the foyer.

While I hadn't had a chance to explore much of the Henson family home, their foyer and ballroom were the definition of extravagant. It wouldn't be much of a leap to assume that their entire home followed the same theme. The marble floors were sparkling even with the amount of traffic I was sure they'd gotten tonight. The staircase was striking, and I could imagine watching Bianca walk down the stairs to greet everyone at this party. There was a large table to the left of the stairs where a beautiful flower arrangement sat. The centerpieces in the ballroom were designed to be smaller versions of this one in the foyer.

"Easton."

I would recognize my mother's voice anywhere. I turned around and came face-to-face with my parents, who were probably wondering why I was staring at a flower arrangement.

"Mom, Dad," I said in return. Their facial expressions didn't give away what they were thinking. Part of me was a little curious, but for the most part I didn't care, because what good would it do?

I expected my father to say something, but I was surprised when my mother spoke up. "Why are you alone? What happened to Nash and Bianca?"

"Nash left the party, and Mrs. Henson took Bianca to introduce her to some people."

My mother nodded. "Ah, Elizabeth seems to be a social

butterfly and the queen of making connections, so I'm not surprised about that. Is everything okay with you?"

I nodded. "I'm good, if not a bit bored."

I watched as Mom tried to hold back a chuckle. When she managed to maintain her composure, she glanced at my father before looking back at me. "I know. That was why I'd hoped you would be able to hang out with some people your own age. It was one of the reasons why we asked you to come tonight. Figured it would be nice for you to meet Nash in person versus whatever text messages you sent back and forth a couple of weeks ago."

Oh, I'd met him alright, but neither of our parents would have been expecting the conversation we'd had. "That makes sense."

"Maybe you guys will be friends by move-in weekend," said Mom.

"Yeah, maybe we will." I had my doubts, but now wasn't the time to discuss them.

"Son."

That one word drew my attention to my father. It felt as if he was scrutinizing every inch of me so hard, I wondered if he would call my bluff.

"The Hensons seem like lovely people, but keep in mind that their son is your competition now."

Nash's thoughts about Bianca and me had made me furious and went beyond him trying to control who she dated. My father's words only fanned the flames within me.

Nash and I would be competing in a few areas now. Football was the obvious one as I knew we both would be playing for the Brentson Bears this fall. But now our social circles would be intertwined, which would make things very interesting.

With me here, would Nash continue to be Brentson's golden boy?

Dad leaned in closer, as if to make sure that no one but the three of us could hear.

"We can talk more about it when we leave because you never know who is listening. You know that we have a reputation to uphold. It might be in your best interest to... what's the saying? Oh yes. Keep your friends close and your enemies closer."

He winked at me, and a small smirk formed on his lips. Dad had said the phrase enough times over the years that we both knew it by heart.

"I understand, Dad."

My father gave me a firm head nod and placed his hand on my shoulder. "Your mother was starting to develop a headache, so we were about to head out. Are you ready to leave?"

It wasn't unheard of for my mother to develop headaches that could go from minor head pain to a migraine, so I didn't blame either of them for wanting to leave. There was nothing left for me to do here anyway. "Yeah. I'm ready."

I looked into the ballroom as we walked toward the front door to see if my eyes would land on Bianca, but apparently it wasn't in the cards. I couldn't find her, and I didn't want to draw attention to myself by trying to do so.

It took several more minutes for us to get our car, but once we were on the road, I watched as my father placed his hand on my mother's. "How are you feeling now, honey?"

"I'm fair. I hate that we had to leave early because of me."

"It's okay. With us establishing a base here, we'll have plenty of opportunities to socialize."

"That's true," my mother said just before she turned her head to look back at me. "Easton, how was your conversation with Nash and Bianca?"

I wasn't surprised that my parents had tabled the conversation about the Henson siblings until we were in the car. "It was fine. Like you said, it was nice to talk to them, and at least I'll know someone at the start of the school year. Did you meet anyone worthwhile this evening?"

My father shifted in the driver's seat before he replied. "We were swarmed a bit with people wanting to introduce themselves to us, and that contributed to your mother's headache."

While I was sure that many of the people at tonight's event were loaded, I had the feeling that we were one of the richest people there, therefore making them one of the most popular couples. My family's wealth had come from investing in a variety of sectors, but the biggest had been in the shipping and the tech industries. The Beaumont family invested heavily in several companies at different levels, including a startup that exploded when it was bought out. We still owned Beaumont Global Logistics as well as several other ventures that our family held interests in that I was vaguely aware of.

I'd made it a point to ignore the family business for now because soon enough, I would be expected to take over from my dad. I tried not to think about the pressure I would have to deal with when the time came.

I'd told my parents multiple times I wasn't sure if I wanted to take over once he retired. It had become a sore point between us. Of course, I should want to take the reins of

Beaumont Global Logistics and the investment portfolio that would eventually be passed down to me. But was that what I wanted to do with my life?

The pressure for me to be my father's successor would be intense, and I wasn't sure if I wanted to live with that. However, I didn't have to worry about that for the time being.

"I mean, I don't blame anyone for trying to talk to you. It's not every day that you come into contact with someone who could potentially finance your dreams and aspirations."

"You're right about that, Son."

Although I couldn't see his face, I could hear the smile in his voice. First and foremost, my father wanted to make money, but if he was able to invest in other people's dreams *and* make money, that made it even sweeter.

My parents' expectations weighed heavily on my shoulders, something that never seemed to get better. It was a steady weight that was almost painful, and I constantly walked through life with it. I'd become used to it to a degree. The only way to relieve the pressure would be to make a decision and face the fallout no matter what.

Instead of facing that issue right now, I turned to look out of the car window and watched as Brentson passed by us in a blur. I couldn't help but wonder if my father would have the same enthusiasm if I didn't want to go into the family business.

But none of those thoughts shifted my attention away from Bianca, the forbidden fruit that I couldn't have.

4

BIANCA

A FEW MONTHS LATER

"Nash, you're supposed to be meeting me at your apartment right now. That was what we decided on." I didn't bother to hide the irritation in my voice.

"I know, I know." The guilt was evident in his voice. "Something came up and I won't be back until late tonight."

That struck me as odd because, as of a few hours ago, our plan was a go. I'd held up my end of the deal and was currently being driven to Nash's place. "Why didn't you mention this before I went on the campus tour?"

This was the weekend that was supposed to give me a taste of what it would be like to be a college student at Brentson University. It started today with us being given a tour of campus, attending a couple of classes, and partaking in several activities. While it had been a long day, I was excited to be here.

Technically, I was supposed to stay on campus, but Dad had pulled a few strings, allowing me to stay with Nash for the weekend. It wasn't done for my benefit though. He just wanted to make sure that nothing I might do this weekend got out to the press. I was shocked he didn't go as far as to have hired a bodyguard.

"Don't you have a football game tomorrow? Getting home late is probably not ideal if you're playing tomorrow."

"Since when did you decide to take over the role of mom? Because our mother, in many ways, refused to be one."

"Damn. That was harsh, Nash."

I heard his sigh through the phone and could sense him shrugging. "You know I'm telling the truth."

He was, but it wasn't something I wanted to get into while a stranger was driving me to my next destination. "So, how am I supposed to get into your apartment?"

"Fuck, I should have given you a key," Nash said but it sounded as if he was muttering it to himself. "I talked to the front desk and told them to expect you, so they should have no issue letting you up."

I sighed. "Okay, but this is so shitty. You know that right?"

"I owe you one."

"This is becoming a running theme with you."

"I know and I promise I'll make it up to you. How was today by the way?"

Nash usually kept his word so I had no doubts that he would now, and he'd been through a lot over the last couple of months. With Raven disappearing without a trace soon after their graduation, I could only imagine the emotions he was feeling so I tried to be more understanding. That didn't mean I wasn't disappointed in this change in events though. "It was great, but I'm exhausted. I should be at your place in a few minutes."

Nash chuckled. "Okay. I'll let you go. If you have any

issues getting into my apartment, call me back. I should be able to answer my phone for the next hour or so."

"Um, that's not strange or anything. Do I even want to know?"

"I couldn't tell you even if you did. I'll see you soon."

"Okay, bye."

I hung up the phone and released a long breath. I appreciated my driver for not trying to start a conversation with me because I didn't want to be chatty right now. I was regretting not driving to Brentson myself. Instead, I turned my attention back to the scenery outside of the car window. Although I got to experience it every year, I swore that I fell more in love with fall in Brentson each year.

October in Brentson meant that the late afternoon light streamed in through the leaves that had turned a variety of colors. While some were still on the trees, many had fallen to the ground. Being a high school senior meant that my schedule was extremely busy, and Nash was a freshman in college, so his wasn't any better. It didn't allow much time to enjoy the change of seasons.

It wasn't much different from having Nash home. His schedule his senior year had been so busy that I rarely saw him. This weekend, I was supposed to be joining him on campus, giving us an opportunity to hang out together. Hopefully, we could after the football game tomorrow.

Before I could blink, we were pulling up to the large building where Nash's apartment was located. I thanked my driver and unbuckled my seat belt. As I opened my door, I was hit with the smell of freshly fallen leaves. It made me yearn for something pumpkin flavored. Maybe I could order food delivery and get something that would satisfy my craving. In the meantime, the driver opened the trunk and exited the vehicle.

I met him at the back of his car, and he handed me the bag I packed for my weekend. I thanked him once more and entered the luxury building that would be my home for the next couple of days.

It took me a second to find the front desk but once I had, I walked over and a woman who looked maybe a little older than me lifted her head with a smile on her face.

"Hello! How may I help you?"

"Hi, I'm staying with my brother this weekend, but don't have a key to his apartment. His name is Nash Henson and he told me to come to the front desk to get everything taken care of."

"And your name?"

"Bianca Henson."

"Do you have any ID on you?"

"Uh—uh, sure." I hadn't been expecting to go through all this, but it wasn't too much trouble. I could understand why they wanted to take precautions. It took some maneuvering, but I was able to grab my wallet and showed my ID.

"It's cool, Melanie," I said after I read the name tag on her shirt. She gave me a small smile because I said her name, and I wondered how many people chose to ignore that. Then again, that could just be presumptuous of me.

She typed on the computer and studied my ID for a moment before handing it back to me. "Okay, Ms. Henson, you're all set. I'll give you some keys and you can return them when your stay is over."

"Sounds good."

Melanie stood up from the desk and walked around to the front. "Do you need any help with your bag?"

"No, I got it." I almost told her I didn't need any help getting to the elevator because I'd been here before, but I let her lead me to the elevator bank.

Melanie summoned the elevator and when the doors opened, she stepped inside, waved the small badge on the keychain, and pressed the number fifteen before handing me the keys.

"Mr. Henson's apartment is 1503. If you need anything, please don't hesitate to call the number on the back of that badge."

"Awesome. Thank you so much."

"You're welcome." With that, Melanie walked out, and the elevator door closed behind her.

I was alone.

For the first time in what felt like days.

While it sucked that Nash wasn't here, maybe this wouldn't be so bad after all.

The elevator ride was quick and once it was over, I walked to Nash's door. It didn't take much effort to get into Nash's apartment, but it wasn't until I'd closed the door behind me that I felt like I could truly relax.

Nash's place was designed to be a sleek and modern space. The natural light that flowed into the living area was to die for and cast a warm glow over both the living room and the kitchen.

I took my bag to the guest room and tossed it on the floor near the bed. I immediately plopped down on the white comforter and fell back, my body slightly bouncing as I settled on the bed. The desire to move anywhere but this very spot was nonexistent.

I shifted my body so that I could pull my phone out of my back pocket. I debated texting my parents to let them know that I was alive and wondered if it was worth it. Reaching out to them right now might stop them from trying to bother me later though, so I typed out a quick message and sent it to both of them.

> Me: Everything went well today, and I'm now back at Nash's apartment for the evening.

Since I already had my phone out, I decided to text my best friend, Iris, too.

> Me: Brentson was pretty cool, and I was able to meet some professors.

> Iris: That's good. I was worried your experience would be like the time we went to camp.

I laughed out loud. Iris and I were not the camping type, but I had begged my parents to put me in a summer camp so I could do something different one summer. I met Iris there, and the rest was history. My parents hadn't been completely thrilled with my friendship with her, but I didn't care.

> Me: No, nothing like that. I wish you were going to come here too.

Iris was a senior this year too and had her heart dead set on going to Westwick University. Thankfully, it wasn't that far from Brentson, but still, it would have been nice for us to be on the same campus.

> Iris: I do too. Speaking of coming there, did you see Easton?

I'd told her about meeting Easton at my parents' party a few months ago, and she asked me about him every so often. Nash and he had grown closer over the summer and had become best friends as far as I knew. However, I'd barely seen him since that evening at my house.

> Me: No, I haven't. That's not surprising though since Brentson University is pretty big, and he has his own thing going on.

I continued to text Iris off and on as the afternoon quickly turned into evening. I'd showered, enjoyed my Chinese takeout and was vegging on the couch when I heard the faint chime alerting me that someone was calling me.

I recognized the name on the screen, but I was slightly confused about why they would be calling me. I accepted the call and put the phone up to my ear.

"Lucy?"

Lucy Brooks and I were friendly, but I wouldn't exactly say that we were friends. She was also a senior at Brentson High. I'd seen her earlier today, visiting Brentson's campus as well. We talked briefly before we continued on our separate ways.

"Bianca! Hey! Come out with us tonight."

"Wait, what?"

"Come out with us tonight! We're going to go to a couple of parties, and I wanted you to come with us."

"Um... why?" I blurted the question out before I could stop myself. This sounded like both an amazing idea and a very bad one all wrapped in one big bow.

"Because it's going to be fun to let loose like we're in college. Come on..."

Her voice trailed off and I wondered if she'd already started drinking. I couldn't deny that I'd wanted an excuse to have a drink tonight but staying here alone had also been nice.

"We have shots of tequila and vodka waiting for you."

That was all the convincing I needed. "Where am I going, and when should I get there?"

Lucy laughed on the other end of the line before she rattled off the address and told me they were getting ready now and would be leaving the dorm they were staying at in about an hour. That didn't give me much time to pull something together, but I could make it work.

Showering earlier made this easier, but the most difficult thing was picking out an outfit for tonight. Luckily for me, I'd thrown some extra clothes in my bag. Since I didn't have many options, it would hopefully make picking out an outfit pretty easy. I picked out a black bra, a sheer shirt, a black blazer, a pair of dark denim jeans, and black boots.

I pulled on my ponytail for a moment before removing my hair tie. My blonde hair fell down slightly past my shoulders and had a natural wave that I could work without having to do much to it. Once I was happy with how it laid, I worked on my makeup, deciding that a lighter smokey eye and red lip was the way to go to tie the look together.

Was this a little much? Would I freeze? Maybe, but there was no turning back now.

After staring at myself for another moment, I packed the small black purse that I brought with me, making sure that I had my brother's keys with me.

I called a car and headed downstairs. Before I knew it, I was whisked back to Brentson University's campus to partake in whatever shenanigans the night would bring.

"I'M SO glad you came tonight!" Lucy exclaimed after she opened the door.

I found myself taken aback. Lucy and I barely hung out in school outside of a few group projects we worked on together, but that might have said more about me than it did about her.

"What's your drink of choice tonight?"

"How did you get all of this?" I said, gesturing to the alcohol that was lined up on an unused desk in the dorm room. I glanced around the room and quickly noticed we weren't alone. I recognized a couple of them from Brentson High, and the rest I'd never seen before. How Lucy had made friends this fast, I didn't know.

She waved me off. "Don't worry about that. We have mixers as well."

Who was I to judge? I had no intention of getting completely shitfaced tonight because I needed to get back to Nash's before he got home. But I did feel awkward being in here with other people I barely knew. Deep down, I knew that I couldn't let my guard down because there was always a chance that word would get out about what I was doing, and things would get back to my parents or to the media. I wasn't sure which one was worse.

"Grab your drink because we're going to head out soon."

Lucy's words cut through my thoughts like a knife, and I was brought back to the present.

I poured a small amount of vodka and mixed it with cranberry juice in a red Solo cup and took a sip. I could barely taste the vodka, but I wasn't going to complain.

"I'm ready whenever you guys are," I said more cheerfully than I felt. I was beginning to wonder why I'd said yes, but I tried to shove those feelings to the side because maybe socializing would be good for me.

We left the dorm room and began to walk to who knew where. Darkness surrounded us, but thankfully, the streetlights on campus provided enough light for us to be able to see. A breeze provided a slight chill in the air as it rustled the tree leaves. At first, I couldn't hear anything, but then I heard the sounds of people chatting and light giggles as they embraced their alcohol-induced haze.

Lucy looked down at her phone and said, "I think the house is down this street and then we need to make a left."

I slowed down enough to take another sip of my drink but once my thirst was quenched, I picked up the pace. When we reached the corner of the block, there was no question that this was where the parties were going on.

Everyone was laughing and drinking, stumbling around, and I couldn't help but shake my head at the scene before me. People watching was so entertaining.

"This way, Bianca!" Lucy called out, bringing a halt to my people-watching party. She was walking up the front steps of a random house, but before she could get to the front door, someone else came stumbling out of it.

"WOOHOO!" the drunk student yelled at the top of his lungs. The group I was with laughed at his antics before he took off running down the stairs. Either he was drunk before he arrived at this house or whatever they were serving here must have been strong.

Lucy opened the door and the first thing we were greeted by was the sound of music pumping out the speakers. As we made our way through the party, I couldn't help but take the atmosphere in. The bass created a steady rhythm that was almost hypnotic. There was no way anyone was falling asleep with the pounding, but it created a trance-like state that brought me to the makeshift dance floor we found in the basement of the house.

I didn't go to many parties that students from Brentson High hosted although I'd been invited to several, but the fun that was being had here made me wonder if I should risk it. Nonetheless, this still made me nervous, and I took a large gulp of my drink to calm my nerves a bit more.

It was becoming very apparent that I was out of my depth, but I wasn't upset about it. So far, no one had made it obvious that they knew who I was. Being able to blend in here was more fun than I was expecting. The weight of my parents' disapproval was lifted for the time being. For tonight, I wasn't the mayor's daughter, and it was amazing. Although there was this nagging pressure point in the back of my mind due to my upbringing, it was as if anything could happen here, and I was embracing it.

"I think we all need a refill!" Lucy darted across the room.

Everyone in our group followed behind her and she

grabbed some more cups to hand out to us. I stuck the new cup into my old cup and walked to the table to see what was available.

There was a reddish liquid on a table with a keg next to it. Before I could decide, Lucy turned and handed me another cup.

"Taste this," she said excitedly. She stood next to me as I grabbed the cup in my other hand and took a sip from hers. The fruitiness hit my tongue first, almost completely masking the sting that I would have assumed would come from the alcohol. Drinking a lot of this could be dangerous, and normally I would have been all for it. But being in a strange place and around people I barely knew had me more cautious.

"I think I'm going to grab some of the beer from the keg over here."

Lucy nodded and moved out of the way so I could get to it. I stared at the keg and froze. I'd seen one in movies but hadn't actually used one before. I preferred the art of stealing my parents' liquor when they weren't around, which was pretty often.

"Need any help?"

I looked at the person who had appeared next to me and my mouth dropped open in shock.

"Uh, yeah sure," I said as he got to work on getting me my beer.

I watched as he masterfully poured the beer from the keg. Once he was done, he handed it to me.

"Thank you, I appreciate it." I was about to walk away, but then his voice stopped me.

"I'm Landon."

Oh, so he wanted to keep this conversation going. "And I'm Bianca."

I mentally slapped myself in the forehead for not giving a fake name. Lucky for me, nothing on his face indicated that my name rang any bells, and I was relieved.

"You're new here? I haven't seen you around."

"Something like that." I flipped my hair back over my shoulder and looked to my right.

My breath left my body and it felt as if I was caught in an invisible grip. My eyes connected with Easton's, much like they had the night of my parents' party. I hadn't expected to see him tonight, although he did appear as a passing thought in my mind earlier. It was as if fate decided that tonight it would have the last laugh. Confusion clouded his face for a split second before his expression became more relaxed as he recognized who I was.

But tonight, things were different.

We weren't at my house.

Neither of our families were here.

And he had another girl curled into his side.

5

BIANCA

When others said everything in the room stopped after something dramatic occurred, I laughed. I thought it was just a bunch of bullshit that people spewed when they wanted to paint a picture that gave you movie vibes. I was convinced it was a way to make something sound more meaningful than it actually was.

I was wrong.

Everything slowed down. The volume of the music lowered to a dull roar. The people that I'd been around were nowhere to be found. Everyone and everything faded into the background. Nothing mattered but the two of us in this moment. If I'd had a slight interest in the guy in front of me before, it had now vanished into thin air.

My reaction to seeing Easton again was unexpected. I'd been unprepared to see him even though I probably should have expected to, but as the shock wore off, something else had taken its place, which I couldn't quite name.

Nothing on Easton's face gave away what he was thinking.

Part of me wished I could read his mind, but I wasn't sure I wanted to know what he was thinking.

The intensity from our stare was enough to make my heart skip a beat. Was he going to come over here or pretend like he hadn't seen me?

I couldn't take it anymore. Ignoring Landon was rude, and if Easton wasn't going to do something, then neither was I. Plus, he should be more than preoccupied with the girl that was currently rubbing her hand down his chest. I pushed my shoulders back and looked away. This was a silly game and a waste of time for both of us.

I took another sip of my beer and gave Landon a tiny smile. "So, Landon, how's the school year treating you?"

"Can't complain so far. The adjustment has been interesting to say the least."

I did a double take. "Are you a freshman?"

Landon nodded and a small smirk appeared on his face. I had a feeling that I knew what he was going to say. "You thought I was older, didn't you?"

My cheeks warmed as my embarrassment sank in. "I'm sorry. I shouldn't have assumed."

"It's not a problem. You're not the first one to think that."

Before I could reply, a hand slid underneath my blazer and along my lower back and I jumped. I glanced to my right, my heart leaping into my throat when I found Easton standing beside me.

I arched one of my eyebrows at him and said, "Can I help you?"

"I was coming over to say hello."

"That doesn't require you touching me."

He ignored my hint to remove his hand from my body. I

could have made a bigger stink about it, but I enjoyed his touch too much to do so.

"You two know each other," Landon said, matter-of-factly.

"We do. I'm Easton," he said as he stuck his hand out to greet Landon.

"Landon. Nice to meet you. We're in Calculus I together."

Easton stared at him for a moment before he said, "That's right, I've seen you before. Apologies, but I'm barely awake during that class."

Landon laughed. "Yes, it is pretty early. If the other sessions hadn't already been filled, I wouldn't have taken it." Landon took a sip from his drink and then said, "I'll let you two go, but I'm sure I'll see you both around."

Landon gave us a small nod and left Easton and me alone. Easton moved and took Landon's place in front of me. He'd created a void within me when he removed his touch, and I hated it. His welcoming smile that he'd given to me when Landon was present, shifted as his eyes narrowed within a second flat. "What the hell are you doing here?"

His change in tone was like whiplash. I didn't know what I was expecting when he got me alone, but it hadn't been that. "That's none of your business. You don't have the right to question me."

Although I was annoyed with him, it took all my concentration to focus on his face and not the white t-shirt that seemed to showcase his muscles. That, paired with the jeans he was wearing, were my kryptonite.

"That's where you're wrong. I can do as I please because now you're on my turf, and we both know you don't belong here. So, explain why you are here. Would calling your brother get me the answers I want? Does he even know you're here, princess?"

I blinked at him once and then twice. I was momentarily too stunned to speak. "Princess? How dare you—"

He cut me off, probably because he knew I was going to sidestep his original question. "For the last time, why are you here, Bianca?"

His demand sent an unexpected tremble through my body, but I did my best to hide it. Instead, I narrowed my gaze at him and said, "I'm here on a college overnight visit, okay? Nash knows I'm on campus because I'm staying with him."

"But he doesn't know that you're here."

I scoffed. "He has to know I'm here if I'm staying at his apartment."

Easton's jaw clenched and I could see that he was trying not to lose his patience. "You know I meant at this party, not just on campus."

I shrugged. "I didn't say that."

He stared at me for a second. "You didn't have to. Your body did. Let's go."

His answer scrambled my brain. He'd been able to read me like that? And what did he mean by let's go? "Wait, what?"

"I'm taking you back to Nash's place."

Easton turned to walk away, but I grabbed his arm to stop him. Nash wasn't going to be able to get any calls for a while, so Easton wouldn't be able to talk to him in real time anyway.

"Why?"

"You shouldn't be here."

That excuse was half-assed, and it was obvious that his attempt to think of something quick had failed. "There's nothing wrong with me being here. I'm not doing anything I shouldn't be."

Easton glanced at the cup in my hand before looking back at me. "You're drinking underage."

"So are you," I said without missing a beat. A small smirk appeared on my face when I realized I had him there.

At first, he looked pleased that I'd gotten the last word, then his expression turned serious.

I spoke before he could. "Some of my friends invited me out, and I'm here to have fun. This is something I rarely, if ever, have gotten to do, and I should be allowed to enjoy it."

Easton looked away, and I wondered what he might be thinking. When he finally turned his head to cast a glance my way, something had shifted in his gaze. "Fine. But you have me stuck to you for as long as we're here."

Conflicting feelings whirled through me as I processed what it meant to have Easton attached to me for the rest of the night. Having an opportunity to be near him again was something I'd thought about repeatedly since the night of the party my parents hosted. On the other hand, I didn't need to be babysat.

I went with the latter. "I don't need a babysitter, Easton. Go on and have fun with your friends, and I'll have fun with mine." I was using the term 'friends' loosely, but he didn't need to know that.

"If you're staying here, then so am I. You don't know much about what goes on here at night, and I don't want to have to deal with explaining to Nash why I didn't stop his sister from doing something stupid when I could have. So, you're stuck with me."

The darkening of his gaze dared me to say something else

about this topic. He'd given me the option of going home or staying here with him by my side. I wanted to take the option that would still allow me to have some fun after getting all dressed up for a night out. "Fine, but I do need to find my friends."

"I'm pretty sure they went to the basement."

Of course, they'd left me up here by myself. At least they hadn't left the house. "Okay, then I guess I'm going to explore the basement."

"It's right over there," Easton said as he pointed in the direction. I looked over my shoulder to see where he was pointing, and then he said, "Lead the way."

I did as he said and led us down into the basement. Lucy and her friends were on the dance floor, seemingly having the time of their lives. When she spotted me on the stairs she waved wildly, showcasing just how drunk she was, and I couldn't help but chuckle. I raised my hand, acknowledging her before continuing down the stairs.

The dimly lit basement was about what I expected when I thought of a place to host a college party. The first thing I was hit with was the air, which was filled with sweat and alcohol. I attributed it to all the dancing and drinking that was occurring down here. Outside of college students everywhere, my eyes landed on the old, mismatched couch and chairs that served only to provide a place to sit versus making an interior design statement. The last time this place had been cleaned out was debatable I decided as I stepped over a couple of red plastic cups.

Due to the volume of the music, it was hard to hear. I had no problem being able to find the DJ that was creating the mood for the party. I moved through the crowd, with Easton making sure that we didn't lose each other. I could feel his touch once more on my lower back, the heat from it causing a jolt of electricity that headed straight to my pussy. I tried to focus on scanning the room and not how close he was to me, when I saw a long folding table with red cups arranged in a triangle on two of its sides. Beer pong would be an interesting game to play.

Easton leaned down and whispered in my ear, his warm breath tickling me and causing the hairs on my arm to stand at attention. "Want to play?"

A sly smile appeared on my face as I turned my head slightly so I could look him in the eye before I nodded. This could be interesting.

With Easton's hand on my lower back, he guided me into the room with the beer pong table. I waited for the people that were currently playing to finish up and leave before I walked over to one end of the table. Easton closed the door most of the way, giving us some privacy and a slightly cozier atmosphere, but maybe it was all in my head. I wanted to ask why he'd done so, but I didn't want to draw attention to it and have him undo what he'd just done.

"Do you know how to play?" he asked as he put both hands firmly on the table.

"Isn't the goal to make sure the ping-pong balls get into the cups?"

"Yes, and let's take a sip of our own drinks if the other gets the ball into a cup because who knows what the hell is in there."

I chuckled even though that was what I was already planning to do. Easton went on to explain a few more rules about how he usually played, which I agreed to, and then it was time for the game to begin.

"Ladies first."

"Remember, this is my first time playing," I said just before I imitated what I thought was the right way to make a shot and let the ball go. I missed the cups in front of Easton by a mile.

Was I slightly embarrassed? Yes, but at least Easton had the common decency not to laugh at my misfortune. When Easton fixed his positioning and lined up his shot, the ball went into one of the cups with ease. I took note of his stance when he lined the shot up the second time and once again, he got the ping-pong ball into one of my cups.

I mumbled under my breath as I shook my head. This might end up being a blowout. I was glad we hadn't bet anything on this game because there was no doubt in my mind that he was going to win the whole game without me being able to score a point.

Thankfully, his next shot missed so it was my turn to throw the ball.

I tried to mimic the way he maneuvered his body this time, and while I'd gotten closer to the goal, I still missed.

"Damn it," I mumbled just before taking a sip of my beer.

"It's okay, Bianca. It's just a game." He didn't say it mockingly or else I might have snapped at him.

"I know but tell that to my competition."

"Trust me when I say I understand that completely."

I knew he did. Since both he and my brother played for the Brentson Bears now, I figured it was embroidered on their DNA at this point.

Easton made a couple of shots in a row once again, and before I could take my turn, his words stopped me.

"Do you want me to help you?"

I debated with myself, well, more so had an argument with my pride before I nodded my head. Easton walked around the table and I held my breath as he stopped behind me.

He stood behind me, molding my body into a position that he thought would be the most beneficial for me to toss the little white ball from. His hands followed the curves of my waist to my hips, lingering for several seconds too long. His touch, although light, set my body ablaze. It was then I was finally able to admit to myself I wanted more, I needed more.

He used his hand to gather my hair so that it was resting over one shoulder instead of down my back, exposing my neck to him.

"Toss the ball."

I could barely hear him over the pounding of my heart in my ears. I closed my eyes for a moment and took in a deep inhale. When I felt slightly calmer, I opened them once more and let the ball fall from my hands.

It landed in one of Easton's cups.

"There you go, princess."

This time it didn't seem as if he was being condescending with the nickname. His praise sounded sincere, and I could feel a moan threatening to slip past my lips.

And this was before his lips touched my skin.

The gasp that fell out of my mouth when he kissed my neck bounced along every wall in this room. My brother's best friend had kissed me, let alone in the basement of a stranger's house. The feel of his lips stayed on my skin as I wished that he would do it again and again and again.

As if he could read my mind, he left a trail of kisses along my neck. I wanted to beg him to kiss me elsewhere too, but I was at a loss for words. When we suddenly heard a loud banging noise, Easton jumped back from me as if I was too hot to touch. I whipped around to look at him, and I could read the look in his eyes immediately.

Regret.

"Bianca, I shouldn't have done that. I'm—"

I put my hand up to stop him. "Save it. I don't want to hear it."

"But—"

I shook my head and rolled my eyes before I caught myself. The moment that we shared together felt as if it had been slammed to the ground and shattered into a million pieces, much like my heart.

"Easton, this has been fun, but I'm going to go."

How I managed to keep my voice steady, I didn't have a clue. While I hadn't had time to process my emotions from this entire encounter, something deep within me forced me not to panic or cry at the rejection I experienced. When I was away from him, I could cry, but I refused to give him the satisfaction of seeing my tears.

"I'll go with you back to Nash's."

"Thanks, but no thanks."

I turned on my heel and took a step toward the door before I felt his hand on my wrist. His hold wasn't tight enough to hurt me, but it would take some tugging for me to break loose from him. I glanced down at where we shared a connection before looking back up into his now stormy green eyes.

"I'll go with you back to Nash's." His voice was firmer this time, not leaving me room to argue with him.

I pulled my wrist free from his grip and he let me go without a fight. I threw my hands up in the air and walked out of the room with the assumption that he was going to follow. When we walked back out into the main part of the basement, I didn't see Lucy or her friends anywhere. With all these people around me and the sound of the music seemingly pouring out of every corner of this basement, I felt completely and utterly alone as I took a couple of seconds to process what had happened between Easton and me.

What I did know was that I needed to get away from him as quickly as possible. If that meant having to deal with him for a few more minutes while he did his "gentlemanly duty" and made sure I was safely back at Nash's apartment, then so be it.

To save even more time, I pulled out my phone once we reached the top of the stairs to call a car. I didn't want to have to awkwardly wait longer for a car to arrive if I didn't have to.

I scanned the main floor of the house to see if I spotted Lucy or any of the other girls, but I came up empty. I assumed they all probably ended up going to another house party while I was playing beer pong with Easton. As if someone had heard my pleas, I noticed the driver who'd decided to pick me up was only a block away, meaning I would have to spend less time with the man of the hour.

Easton walked around me and opened the door for me. I mumbled a quick thank you as I walked through the door, and just as we hit the porch, a car pulled up to the front of the house.

"Is that the car?" he asked.

"Think so," I said as I showed him the license plate. Easton walked ahead of me again and walked toward the back of the car while the driver rolled down his window.

"Bianca?" he asked, and I nodded.

During this time, Easton walked back around toward the car door nearest me and opened it. He gestured for me to get in and he walked around to get in on the other side. Once Easton was seated with his seat belt on, the driver pulled away from the curb.

I had no intention of starting a conversation with anyone in this car and maybe it was due to the vibes that I was giving off, but neither guy tried to talk to me, and I was grateful for that. I didn't want to pretend to be friendly right now, instead choosing to withdraw into myself until I was ready to face the world again.

The ride to Nash's apartment was quiet. As soon as the car pulled to a stop outside of the building, I broke the silence. "Are you going to take me up to the front door as well?"

Easton looked at me for a split second before undoing his seat belt and stepping out of the car. I took my seat belt off as he opened my door. I thanked my driver and walked into Nash's building with Easton right behind me. I gave the person working at the front desk a polite smile as we walked to the elevator bank.

Easton and I stepped into the elevator and made it up to Nash's floor in complete silence. I was just a few seconds away from escaping his presence.

When we reached Nash's door and I unlocked it, I looked over my shoulder at Easton and said, "I don't want to talk about this night ever again."

"Deal. This night never happened."

"I'll see you around." *Not if I could help it.*

Before Easton could say another word, I closed the door behind me. Once I heard the click of the door confirming I locked it, I exhaled a deep breath that felt as if it left my lungs without an ounce of air. I made a list in my head about what I needed to do before I could fall asleep.

I whipped off the blazer I had on just as there was a knock on the door.

What the hell?

I walked back to the door and looked through the peephole and confusion muddled my thoughts. I unlocked the door and yanked it open.

"What are you doing—"

The rest of my words vanished into thin air because Easton's lips were smashed against mine.

6

BIANCA

Everything in my brain short-circuited when his lips touched mine, and I wasn't even sure if we'd locked the door. If Nash came home right now, we were fucked, but we'd cross that bridge when we got to it.

Any brain power that was left was focused completely and utterly on Easton. From the way he was touching me to the way he was making me feel. He shifted his hands across my body, touching every part of me that he could.

Excitement and fear about what was to come crowded my senses. Doubts about whether I could do this smacked every corner of my brain before I quieted them. This was something I'd wanted to do for months now, and I wasn't about to let self-doubt ruin it for me.

Easton broke our kiss long enough to rip my blazer from my hands and study my body as if committing it to memory. My sheer shirt left little to the imagination although I could see the wheels in Easton's head turning as he took in every inch that had been revealed to him.

Easton pulled me to him and this time, he grabbed my

ass, groaning as he pulled me closer to his body. But it was only momentarily. When he broke away from me again, my heart sank in my body.

As if he could read my thoughts, he said, "I'm not stopping this time, princess. Unless you want me to."

I had no intention of telling him to stop. I swear if he ended any of this before we were both ready, I was going to scream.

"Do you want me to stop, Bianca? This is your last chance. I need to hear you say the words."

"I don't want you to stop." *Ever.*

He grabbed my hand and together, we quickly walked to the guest bedroom where Easton closed and locked the door behind us. Thankfully, I'd left the lamp on when I left for the night, giving us plenty of light to see with.

Easton ate up the distance between us with one step and his hands landed on the sides of my face. I searched his eyes to see if I could see any signs of rejection, but I found none. His stare had darkened considerably, and I knew it was because of me.

He kissed me again, this time more sensual versus the passionate kiss we shared at the door. It was as if he'd completely lost control moments ago and now he'd regained it, at least momentarily.

His hands moved down my body until his fingertips danced along the hem of my sheer shirt. When I felt him grip the material, I lifted my arms so that he could quickly remove it from my body. When the only thing standing between him and my breasts was the black bra that I'd thrown on earlier this evening, my nerves became more frayed. This was really happening.

"I was debating peeling your jeans off you, but I think I would rather watch you do it. That bra of yours is barely going to contain your tits and I'm going to enjoy every second of it."

I swallowed hard as my hands made their way to my waistband. I unbuttoned the top button and slowly pulled the zipper on my pants down. Although I was nervous as hell, I stared into his green eyes as I slowly pushed the denim down my legs, giving him a full show as I bent over until my jeans touched my ankles.

His gaze refused to move from my chest until I straightened my body and stepped out of my pants and boots. I was now left in my matching black bra and thong, which I was now so damn happy I packed. He reached forward and took my lips once more, this time eliciting a moan from my mouth.

It was as if the sound was music to his ears because his kiss became rougher. Something snapped inside of him, and he needed to have me now.

My hands came up to rest on his chest, clenching the fabric of his shirt between my fingers. I, too, was desperate for him.

Easton left small kisses on my lips before gently biting my lip. I gasped at the new sensation before he let it go, taking the opportunity to kiss me hard again. However, this time, his tongue joined the private party our mouths were having.

His taste was intoxicating. It was a mixture of the alcohol he'd had that night and something that was uniquely him. It was something I couldn't get enough of, but there was something I wanted more.

I pulled away from Easton and said, "I think you have on too many clothes."

"Is that right?" he asked as an amused smile formed on his lips.

"Yes," was the only word I could form as I watched him move one of his arms toward his back and pull his shirt off in one smooth motion. I was now left wondering if that might have been the hottest thing I'd ever seen, but Easton didn't give me too long to host the debate with myself.

"Strip. I want the rest of your clothes off." His voice was nothing more than a harsh whisper, as if he was struggling to maintain his sanity.

My hands shook slightly as they made their way to the clasp that held my bra closed. I was slightly distracted by his hands as they made their way to his waistband. I was momentarily paralyzed when I watched him unbuckle his belt with one hand. As he undid his pants, his eyes never diverted to anything else, like they were searching for something within me.

After he was left in only a pair of black boxer briefs, he said, "Bianca?"

The way my name flowed off his tongue was like a warm caress, but also served as a warning that I was supposed to be doing something as well. I shrugged my shoulders to get a better angle on my bra, forcing one of the straps to fall slightly. Easton watched the strap before I undid my clasp. Before the bra could fall, I moved my hands so I could secure the bra to my chest.

"I want to see you. Every part of you. You never need to think or fear that you have to hide from me."

A sharp inhale was my response to Easton's declaration. It took a couple of seconds for me to comply and let the piece of clothing fall from my chest and down to the floor.

Easton swallowed hard. "You're fucking beautiful."

A flush appeared across my body as his words warmed me, but when he walked toward me and pulled me into his arms, it felt as if my body had gone up in flames. He backed me up until my legs hit the bed and I fell back. He watched as my breasts jiggled from the motion and his gaze darkened even more. I watched as he climbed onto the bed with me, his body hovering over mine.

He briefly kissed my lips again and I could feel my panties growing wetter by the second. He left a trail of kisses along my neck and jaw, finding a particularly sensitive spot on my neck. I gasped and arched into his touch, wanting more of what he was willing to give. When I felt his cock brush up against me, my eyes widened. It was as if it was teasing me about what was to come, and while I was nervous, I also couldn't wait.

His hands made their way to my breasts. He played with my nipples until they turned hard as pebbles, before sticking one of them into his mouth. The sensations that coursed through me weren't like anything I'd felt before. He took his time, making sure to give equal attention to both tits. I closed my eyes as I embraced everything that he was doing to me. It felt so good that I could cry.

"Do you want this to be fast or slow?"

I was surprised at his question. Images of having a significant other that made love to you slowly and tried to ease the pain of losing one's virginity appeared and quickly vanished from my mind. Part of me wanted to save and savor every second of this moment, but the other part of me was desperate for him right now.

"Fast," I said with more confidence than I felt.

"I was hoping you would say that. Spread your legs."

With no preamble, he moved one hand down my body where it rested on my panties. As I took another breath, he moved his hand to give himself more access to my pussy. When I thought that he might continue to play with me over my panties, he changed things up. He wasted no time in moving them to the side.

"Fuck, you're already so wet," he said. "I need a taste."

Easton quickly did away with my panties and moved his body so that he was positioned between my legs. It wasn't until our eyes connected that he bent down and laid a kiss on my inner thigh before moving to the other.

I trembled in anticipation of what he was going to do next.

He ran a finger up and down my slit before slipping one digit into my pussy. I gasped at the intrusion. He waited a beat before he began to move. My back arched in response as I gripped the sheets to give my hands something to do. He pulled his finger out just before he ran his tongue along my clit. No matter how hard I tried to fight every emotion I felt, I failed. I ended up crying out instead, letting Easton know the effect he was having on me.

This time I was the one to break our eye contact because I couldn't take it anymore. I let go of the sheets and my hands found their way into Easton's hair, anchoring his mouth to my cunt.

He gave me what I wanted and then some before he suddenly stopped. I froze before I opened my eyes and found him standing at the end of the bed digging through his pants. He produced his wallet and then quickly grabbed the condom that he must have stashed in there.

I watched as he pulled down his boxer briefs and my eyes widened at the sight. How was that going to fit—

My thoughts died as Easton climbed back on the bed with a wrapper in hand. Once he covered himself with the condom, I held my breath in an effort to hide how anxious I was.

This was it. This was really happening.

"Is this what you want?"

I took in a deep breath. "Yes. Absolutely. One hundred and fifty percent."

I moved my legs slightly to give him more room, which he wholeheartedly took. He rubbed his dick up and down my slit before I felt the head of his cock slide just past my entrance. He waited a moment before he sunk into me, his eyes following my every move.

My eyes squeezed shut as the pleasure I felt turned into pain. I was afraid to open my eyes because of what I might see on his face. My body tensed up and I bit back the cry I wanted to shout out. There was no way I was going to be able to hide from him a second longer.

"Look at me," his voice made it sound as if he was barely holding on.

I did as he demanded. His eyes searched my face before they narrowed. "We have a few things we need to discuss, princess."

I knew we did, but it could wait until after we were done. "I think we're preoccupied with something at the moment that I would prefer to see all the way through."

He took that as his incentive to continue, and when he moved, I cringed slightly as my body adjusted to his dick. The more he moved, the pain lessened as my body relaxed and pleasure began to flow through me once more.

"Please don't stop," I begged, and he rewarded me with thrusts that forced his name to the tip of my tongue. I wrapped my legs around him, forcing him to sink deeper into me. The change from pain to ecstasy was erotic in a way that I wasn't expecting but had come to crave.

In this moment, I was his and he was mine.

While what he was doing was tipping me toward the edge, I wanted more. I squeezed my legs around his waist and said, "I'm not some porcelain doll that you need to carry gently. I wanted you to fuck me harder."

That seemed to push him into another gear and his strokes became more determined, as if he was a man on a mission to satisfy us both.

Our gazes clashed once more, and I refused to look anywhere else but at him. Right now, he was the only thing that mattered and the only thing I could think about was the impending climax that was building within me.

This felt more intense than any orgasm I'd ever given myself.

My back arched as I fell over the cliff of orgasmic bliss. Easton leaned forward and took my nipple in his mouth as my body tried to make sense of what was happening to it.

A low growl turned into a loud groan as his thrusts became more erratic. "Fuck," he said as his thrusts slowed down until he completely stopped.

Easton leaned down and rested his forehead on mine as he tried to catch his breath. His eyes were closed for a moment before they sprang open, and I was looking into the storm that I'd created in them.

"Kiss me," I said.

A predatory look returned to his eyes as he kissed my lips once more.

"Now, I want you to lay down so I can finish what I need to do. Then we'll talk."

Instead of arguing with him, I did as I was told, and by the time I was settled on the bed, he'd returned with a washcloth. When the warm cloth touched my pussy, I almost snatched it out of his hand.

"Let me do this, princess."

Regret about not telling him I was a virgin before we fucked sat on my brain like a double-edged sword. His insistence on taking care of me made me feel slightly worse, but being pampered like this was lovely.

What I wasn't ready for was the talk we were supposed to have afterward.

He finished cleaning me up and then he took care of himself. When he finished up in the bathroom, he walked around the bed and slid beneath the covers.

I nearly jumped out of my skin when Easton's body curled around mine. He moved my hair out of the way, and I could feel his soft breath tickling the back of my neck. Goose bumps formed on my skin, and I buried myself deeper into the bedding.

"Why didn't you tell me?"

I scrambled to find an answer but came up empty. "I'm not sure."

That was a lie. I knew why I'd decided not to tell him, but it would probably make me look like an idiot if I admitted it out loud.

Easton let his finger trace small circles on my arm. "Did

you think I wouldn't understand? Or that I'd judge you for it?"

I sighed and said, "I didn't want you to stop because of my inexperience. I wanted this more than anything, and I was afraid to ruin the moment."

His silence was as loud as a freight train as I waited for him to say something. Anything.

"I wouldn't have thought any less of you. I might have taken my time a bit more and tried to ease you into it, but your lack of experience doesn't change the way I view you."

The anxiety that had been sitting in the pit of my stomach loosened. I sighed as the tension I felt left my body. "I'm sorry, I—"

"You don't have to say sorry, but next time something like this happens, I want you to tell me everything."

I turned over and he moved to accommodate me. We ended up with me laying my head on his chest. "Next time?"

"Next time," Easton confirmed.

"Thank you," I whispered. "For being so kind about this and understanding."

"It was my pleasure."

I giggled at Easton's response because he'd without a doubt brought me a whole lot of pleasure. As soon as I stopped, a yawn escaped from my mouth just as Easton's arms tightened around me.

The longer I laid still listening to Easton's heartbeat, the more exhaustion slowly took over, and the events of the entire day took their toll.

"It's time for us to get some sleep," he whispered as he placed a kiss on my forehead and turned off the lamp that I'd left on earlier that night.

With the room shadowed in darkness, I sighed and shifted my body until I once again found a comfortable spot for my head on his chest.

Within moments, I drifted off into a peaceful sleep, unaware of what tomorrow would bring.

7

BIANCA

I blinked my eyes and groaned as I tried to wake from my slumber. The light that was coming in from the curtains made it difficult to see. I was slightly disoriented and confused about where I was. Why wasn't I in my own bed or in my own room? Memories of yesterday came flooding back and everything started to make sense. I was in Nash's apartment, sleeping in his guest room because I was staying at Brentson University for the weekend. Then the events of last night played like a movie in my head and it almost felt as if my heart dropped.

Easton and I had slept together last night.

I was no longer a virgin.

Fuck. Panic rose in my chest as I thought of what would happen if Nash were to find out what we did. I was convinced that my older brother was going to kill me. I'd fucked his best friend and I liked it. What the hell had we done?

Speaking of his best friend, I turned over to find that I was in bed alone. I couldn't hide the disappointment when I realized that he wasn't here. When had Easton left? Had it all been a dream?

I whipped the covers off my body and stretched. The aches that I felt confirmed that this wasn't a dream. I checked my phone and found one text message from Lucy asking if I'd had a good night, but that was it.

With a heavy sigh, I stood up and looked back at the bed. I could still feel his touch on me. Although I longed for his embrace again, it was probably best that he wasn't here. Nash would lose his mind if he'd found Easton and me in bed together. Easton and I didn't talk about what would happen after last night and I was now regretting that. Questions swirled in my brain as I wondered if this was just a one-night stand or something more.

Did I even want something more?

I had no way of contacting Easton unless I went through Nash. We'd never exchanged phone numbers and unless he'd hidden it somewhere, he didn't leave a note for me to read.

What would Nash's reaction be if he found out? He was bound to want to kill both of us so did it even matter? How could I be so stupid as to fuck his best friend?

What the fuck had I been thinking?

No, the issue was that I hadn't been thinking at all.

I stood up and immediately went into the guest bathroom. I was thankful for whoever was the designer of this unit who decided that there should be an additional door that connected the guest bathroom and bedroom. That way, I didn't have to walk into the hallway and run into anyone before I was ready. I needed to pull myself together at least somewhat before I would be able to face whatever the world was about to throw at me head on.

While I showered, I ran through all the possible scenarios that I could about the situation I'd willingly put myself into. None of the solutions I came up with seemed like the right one, and I wasn't sure what to do.

Maybe I shouldn't be thinking so hard about this. After all, I wasn't the only person involved, and at the end of the day, I needed to talk to him so we could come to an agreement on what would happen next.

Once I left the shower and dried myself off, I tossed on a black t-shirt and a pair of black jeans that had an intentional designer hole over one of the knees. I tossed my hair into a ponytail and applied some light makeup.

It was still somewhat early, but there were a few events I was supposed to attend on campus today and it didn't hurt to have a head start and be ready to go now.

When I walked back into the guest room, I found my black blazer lying on the dresser. I moved it and found the rest of the clothes I wore last night folded neatly under it.

So, he had come back in here at some point and picked up my clothes. That would make it easier to hide what happened between the two of us. If Nash had noticed my blazer strewn about, he would've had questions about what I got up to last night.

Thank goodness Easton thought this through because I might have been screwed otherwise.

I walked over to the door that would lead me to the rest of the apartment and took a deep breath before I twisted the doorknob.

This was it, the moment of truth.

I hesitated for a moment before I left the bedroom and walked into the living area. I was greeted by the sight of Nash sitting on the couch, quietly watching television. He looked up when he noticed I walked into the room.

"Hey, Bianca. Did you have a good night last night?"

It took everything in me to school my face so I didn't have a strange reaction to his comment. I made my way into the kitchen to get something from the fridge because it served as an excuse to avoid eye contact with Nash. "Yeah, it was a pretty quiet night. Missed hanging out with you though."

He exhaled loudly. "Yeah, I'm sorry about all of that. If I could have skipped it, I would have."

"And you're still not going to tell me what was up or why it was so important?" I closed the fridge after realizing there was nothing in there that I wanted.

"Nope. And it's not because I don't want to. It's because I can't."

I turned to look at him, this time feeling more confident because the focus wasn't on me. He returned my stare and then something clicked within me. "This isn't about the Chevaliers, is it?"

While I knew very little about the secret society that both my father and grandfather had been a part of, I did know that they both joined during their freshman year at Brentson University, meaning that the timing would be right for Nash to be looking into joining too.

"Easton should be here any second and then we—"

His words were cut off by a knock on the door. Nash had been saved from my questions by Easton's arrival, but now I felt as if I was being thrown into the gauntlet. If what Nash was saying was true, why couldn't it be anyone else at the door?

Part of me wanted to run back into the guest bedroom

and close the door behind me, but if that didn't raise red flags, nothing would.

A feeling of unease tossed together with excitement flew through my body as I watched Nash stand up from his seat. I steadied myself as I watched him walk over to the door and open it without another thought. In walked Easton with a gym bag thrown over his shoulder. I watched as he smiled warmly at Nash before his gaze landed on me.

For a split-second Easton's gaze softened, and I saw a glimpse of the tenderness he'd done his best to show me last night. But that moment didn't last.

The shift in his body language was subtle, but it hit me like a hammer to the face. I could see the hesitancy in his eyes that quickly grew more intense. The tension in the air was thick and it wouldn't take much for it to be set ablaze.

I tried to convince myself that I was overthinking this, but deep down, I knew I wasn't. Something was very wrong.

"Hi, Bianca."

Even the way he said my name was strange. There was no trace of the intimacy from the night before. There was nothing there in his voice but stoicism.

As my hope vanished, I couldn't stop my heart from shattering into a million and one pieces.

Without so much as a second glance, Easton turned to Nash and said, "We need to head to the field now to prepare for today's game."

I didn't want to think that he'd casually dismissed me, but the feeling was there. I refused to give anything away and kept my face blank.

Nash nodded his head slowly before he replied, "Okay, let

me just throw a couple more things into my bag and then I'll be good to go."

With that, he left the room, leaving Easton and me alone. I knew I needed to work fast to get to the bottom of this.

"So about last night..."

My voice trailed off as I waited with bated breath. It wasn't the best way to start this conversation, but it was the only way I could think of doing it.

"It didn't happen."

I licked my lips as I tried to control my emotions. I'd been transported to an alternate dimension because there was no way that this was happening. My hands shook slightly from the rage and hurt that was growing. I couldn't yell or scream right now and that's all I wanted to do.

"It most definitely did, Easton. There is no need to be an asshole about this."

"It meant nothing to me."

"Now, I know that's a lie."

Easton shook his head sharply as if he was growing frustrated with me. "Bianca, don't make me say it."

"No, say it. Say how you feel and then I'll leave you alone." My voice was just above a whisper, but my anger dripped from every word.

The green eyes that brought me such warmth last night, were now as cold as ice. "You were nothing more than an easy fuck. Nothing more, nothing less."

My lips trembled as I closed my eyes. I wouldn't let him see me cry. I wouldn't let him see me cry. With a deep breath, I opened my eyes, looked into his, and said, "The only thing that I want you to do is not tell anyone about last night. Especially not my brother. That's the bare minimum you could do for me."

Easton nodded. I held out my hand for him to shake and when he did, I ignored the buzzing I felt from touching him again. It was then that I decided that I couldn't be in the room with him any longer. I turned on my heel and left the room. I thought I might have heard Easton whisper something that sounded like goodbye, but I wasn't sure. I also wasn't about to turn around to find out.

Just as I was about to enter the guest room, Nash exited his room and looked at me with a bright grin.

"Are you going to come and watch us play today?"

I thought about it for a second and said, "I'll try. Maybe I'll meet up with a couple of friends and they'll come along too."

"Excellent, I'll see you later."

I walked into my bedroom for the weekend and shut the door behind me. The tears that I'd done my best to hold onto were in freefall down my face, but I managed to remain quiet until the front door slammed closed.

I grabbed the closest thing to me, my comb, and flung it at the wall. The sound as it made contact did little to calm me down.

I threw myself down on the bed as the weight of the situation fell on my shoulders. There was no way that I could ever see Easton again, but then again, it wasn't as if I could avoid him. Nash and he had grown close over the last few months, and while I could avoid him after this weekend for a while, eventually I'd be attending Brentson as well. This was nothing but an awkward, tension-filled mess that I now had to live with.

I was such a fucking idiot.

I buried my face in my hands, giving my tears another place where they could land. The words he whispered in my ear last night almost felt like a figment of my imagination, but my body told me that everything was real.

Nothing remained but the memories of bliss that had now been replaced by the sting of sorrow.

8

EASTON

Sleep should have overtaken me a long time ago, yet here I was, staring up into darkness, with nothing but my thoughts to keep me company. The shadows on my walls danced as if they were at a rave, openly mocking me for what I'd done. Closing my eyes should have gotten rid of the problem, but it didn't.

I should have been happy. After all, we'd won our game earlier today, and I'd partied way too hard after it. I did have a slight headache, but that wasn't the reason I was awake.

I'd gone to bed hours ago, yet I tossed and turned all night. When I looked out my window, I was slowly watching the beginnings of the sun starting to rise. If I didn't fall asleep soon, the sun would be greeting me and my only saving grace was that today was Sunday.

And yet sleep still eluded me.

Fortunately, I knew what the cause was.

I was a fucking liar.

The act of admitting it to myself didn't hurt as much as it

should have. That could be due to how many times I'd repeated it to myself since it happened.

I lied straight to Bianca's face. Even though she probably hated me, that would be easier than telling her about the agreement her brother and I reached. Besides my attraction to her, the fact that she was off-limits due to the deal between Nash and me made her even more enticing. Not to mention, being with me would be detrimental to her and her future, and I didn't want to put her through that.

The hurt that radiated from her blue eyes as I spoke those words to her was enough to burn. Every expression that crossed her face as I spoke was etched in my memory despite how hard she tried to hide them from me. However, it was obvious that she was holding back tears and that killed me. I wasn't sure how I would ever remove the memories. The guilt that came along with what I said hadn't lessened an ounce either, making it very hard to pretend that everything was okay. Replaying the look on her face when I said the words that turned me into a liar was what would haunt me forever.

Not only had I lied to her, but I'd lied to Nash as well. Technically with him, it was a lie by omission, but it was a lie, nonetheless. I made a promise that I wouldn't pursue anything with her, and then, being that close to her again along with seeing that she clearly wanted to see what could happen between us too, I couldn't resist even though I should have. Now there were bigger issues at stake than the state of Nash's and my relationship.

At least I'd made sure to find the clothes we dropped along the way and cleaned up the mess we made before I left Bianca tucked in tight in her brother's apartment. If I hadn't, there would have been a whole lot of questions we would have needed to answer immediately.

Hell, maybe that would have made things easier in the long run. But I would never know the answer to that.

"I'm such an asshole," I said to myself. It felt like there was no way out of this, and while keeping quiet was a temporary solution, there was still a chance for the truth to be unearthed.

Without a doubt, I should have never made that promise to Nash. Or, since I had, I should have listened to my subconscious that warned me to walk away when I had the chance.

But I couldn't resist the urge to touch every inch of her.

And that's what had gotten me into trouble.

In an effort to quiet my brain, I rolled onto my side and closed my eyes. Once again, it was to no avail. I couldn't escape the memory of my night with Bianca. The way her body felt against mine. The way she looked when she came.

I would never experience that again, and there wasn't a thing I could do about it now.

I rolled onto my back because it was more enticing than lying on my side. She was all I could think about as I stared at my ceiling. I allowed the pain that I felt to continue to eat away at me. It had been almost a day since Bianca and I last spoke, but it felt as if the moment had happened only minutes ago.

"Maybe telling her the truth would have been the smarter option," I thought out loud, and let the idea sit out there, unchallenged. Taking back what I said was an option, but there was a chance that she still wouldn't want to talk to or see me ever again.

I ran a hand through my hair and shook my head. Telling

her the truth now was pointless and would only cause another opportunity for Nash to be suspicious about why I would want to see his sister alone so we could chat.

No, staying away from her was the best idea.

In the end, she would realize this was the best choice for both of us and our futures. It was the way things needed to be done. The way they needed to be.

At least that was what I told myself.

I rubbed my hands along my face to relieve the tension. The only way to get over this was to forget about it and her, no matter how hard it would be. Though we'd have to see each other eventually, and I was sure neither one of us was looking forward to that.

After deciding that staring at my ceiling wasn't a good use of my time, I snatched the covers off my body and stood up. The clock on my nightstand told me that it was 6:45 a.m., way too fucking early to be awake, but here I was.

My bare feet briefly felt cool on the wooden floor as I left my bedroom to go into the kitchen. My parents wouldn't have Nash outdo me by having an apartment off campus, so I did as well. Something that I couldn't explain coursed through me, and before I could stop myself, I slammed a fist against the wall.

"Fuck," I said as I winced through the pain. I'd hoped that hitting the wall would help me feel something other than guilt, but it only lasted for a split-second.

I walked into my kitchen and grabbed a glass to pour some water into. Dehydration wouldn't help my efforts to fall asleep either. As I drank from my mug, my eyes landed on the small balcony that I hadn't had the opportunity to use since I moved into my place.

Some fresh air could do the trick and make it easier for me to fall asleep. I took my cup to the glass sliding doors and opened them. I was greeted by a cool breeze that made me regret not putting more clothes on before I stepped out onto the balcony.

The air felt refreshing and, for a moment, everything was right in the world.

I sipped my water as I gazed out at Brentson as the city began to wake up. I couldn't help but wonder if Bianca had easily fallen asleep tonight or if she was up watching the sunrise, having not caught a wink of sleep either.

The fresh air's effect on me didn't last long. I still didn't feel better. The lies that I told were hurtful, and that was on purpose. If she hated me, then maybe it would make it easier for her to get over all of this.

I went back and forth, thinking about whether I would take back our time together if given the opportunity. Although my response should be that I would in order to make the outcome between Bianca and me better, I couldn't. I enjoyed her trusting me enough to give me the opportunity to worship the fuck out of her body while I had the chance.

Watching her fall apart in my arms was like nothing I'd ever experienced before, and with everything in me, I wanted to relive the experience.

But that was off the table and in the depths of hell at this point.

"Easton, get your shit together," I muttered to myself before I took another drink from my mug. I felt guilty about taking her virginity because I didn't deserve to be her first. She'd entrusted something to me that she shouldn't have. She deserved so much more than the twisted fuck up I was.

Because there were so many things that she didn't know about me.

I should have walked away from this entire situation when I had the chance. With a heavy sigh, I took my now empty mug and strolled back into my apartment, closing myself off to the outside world once more.

I put the mug into the sink because I'd decided that I had no intention of cleaning it until I tried to sleep again. Thankfully, I was feeling somewhat tired now, so the water and standing outside had done the trick. When I walked back into my bedroom, I made sure that my blackout curtains were completely closed and I turned off my phone, hoping to prevent waking up anytime soon.

Once I was back in bed, even though I tried to avoid it, my thoughts were still on Bianca. I made a promise to myself that I would only allow thoughts of her until I woke up. After that, I would lock the memories of her into the deepest corner of my mind and throw away the key.

I made another promise to myself that I would stay the hell away from her.

Then again, I wasn't any good at keeping my promises.

9

BIANCA
PRESENT DAY

"Shots!"

I jumped and clapped my hands together. This moment had been building within me since the last shot I took.

"Are you ready?"

I grabbed the shot glass that was placed in front of me and nodded almost as quickly as I was clapping. I was already several drinks deep and couldn't wait to add this one to my body. After all, that's what tonight was all about.

I put the shot glass in front of me and then placed my hands around my back. With just my mouth I leaned forward with my mouth open wide. I wrapped my lips around the shot glass and tipped my head back, swallowing the alcohol in one big gulp.

Vodka.

My old tried and true.

The liquid provided a warmth I couldn't replace. It made being in this room full of people bearable. I forced a smile on my face as I twirled around. Hearing people cheering for me as I drank provided an adrenaline rush that I couldn't describe.

The clapping from my sorority sisters cheered me on as I did another small dance. It was as if I was on cloud nine.

Yet it only lasted for a few seconds before I was again ready to be alone in my apartment, away from the rest of the world. Instead, I was at the center of a party at Eta Sigma Nu, the sorority I pledged to during the spring semester of my freshman year.

Someone grabbed my arm, and I looked up to find Taylor, one of my sorority sisters, standing beside me. "This might be the best party that we've ever thrown!"

Even in my drunken state I could see that Taylor's eyes were glassy. She and I must have been riding the same wave because I suspected that my gaze probably looked similar. I wondered how much she had to drink tonight.

"It might be," I said with my fake smile. Most of the parties that I attended nowadays blended together, so it was hard to tell where one started and another one ended.

Here I was in a crowded room, surrounded by friends and acquaintances alike, yet I still felt like I didn't quite belong. It wasn't as awkward as the fundraisers I'd attended with my family over the last couple of years, but the feeling that I shouldn't be here still persisted. With it now being the beginning of my sophomore year, you would think I would be used to this, but there was still something missing.

I didn't have much I needed to worry about. Outside of my studies and grades, I was involved in my sorority and their foundation, hung out with friends, and partied hard. To others, my life was perfect, but on the inside, I felt lost. I attributed it to my age and the stage in my life, but I wasn't sure.

I shook the feeling off and kept dancing. After all, I needed to play my part as the life of the party. The party continued for hours, and over time, a headache began to form. When I checked my phone and saw that it was after two in the morning, I knew I had to get home. I made my way through the crowd and with each step I took, the headache became more pronounced. When I made it through the throng of bodies, everything became a blur as I tried to figure out the world around me.

I gasped when my eyes landed on the man that I'd been intentionally trying to avoid for almost two years. I closed my eyes for what had to be several seconds and then opened them again. But he wasn't there. Had I just imagined it?

I shook my head slightly and it did nothing to clear my alcohol laden fog. I wasn't sure how I did it, but after a few wobbly steps, I managed to make it to the front door. I sidestepped a couple that was making out and opened the door, where I was greeted by a cool breeze. The relief I felt on my warm skin was more than welcomed.

I steadied myself by holding onto the railing. My eyes snapped shut as I waited for the dizziness to fade away.

"Bianca?"

I turned to the person who said my name. It took me some time to be able to get my eyesight to focus, but once I did, I was able to make out that it was Lucy.

"Hey," I said slowly, trying to seem more sober than I actually was. "How are you doing?"

I wasn't sure if I was slurring my words, but she came up to put an arm around my shoulder.

"Do you need a ride home? I haven't been drinking tonight because I have a huge test coming up."

I nodded my head and wished I hadn't, but it got the point across. She walked me to her car and then helped me into the passenger seat. I immediately rolled down the window because I was worried about throwing up.

Somehow, I managed to keep myself together, and the drive to my place wasn't too bad. I thanked Lucy and managed not to embarrass myself too much before I got into my apartment. Once Lucy was gone, I laid on my couch and closed my eyes, enjoying the silence that surrounded me. But that only lasted for a minute.

Because I'd passed out.

MY HANGOVER WAS SEVERE. I felt like an idiot for drinking so much. One would think I would have learned my lesson, but I knew I hadn't. I would be drinking a shit ton of alcohol again soon.

And I deserved a pat on the back for not throwing up this time.

After collecting the food that I ordered from the door, I checked my phone and realized I hadn't talked to Iris in a couple of days. Without a second thought, I called her and waited to see if she would respond.

"Hey," Iris said.

"Hey yourself." Although we'd known each other for years, I would say over the last couple, we'd become best friends.

"I'm shocked you called me."

I rolled my eyes at her even though she couldn't see it through the phone. "Decided to do something different. Are you settled in at Westwick?"

I hadn't talked to her since she'd been back on campus. I would have called her earlier, but I was busy sleeping off the hangover from the night before. To be honest, I didn't want her to know how much of a hot mess I was, and calling her when I was in a zombie state would have easily given it away.

"Yeah. Well, things could be better, but I won't complain too much. Heading to grab some food before everything shuts down."

"Spill. Do I need a glass of wine?" I was joking because there was no way I could drink anything besides water right now.

She scoffed. "No. You shouldn't be drinking alcohol anyway."

It sounded as if she was teasing, but I couldn't help but wonder if I was doing as good of a job at hiding how much I was drinking as I'd thought.

I shoved away the feelings that I had about what she said and continued talking. "Never stopped me anyway. I won't get anything, but you're not getting out of this. Tell me what's up."

While I waited for her to speak, I shoved a forkful of pasta into my mouth. The carbs were helping me to not feel like death, and I was grateful for that.

"It's nothing too serious. My laptop is being a pain in the ass and I'm hoping that doesn't mean it's going to die soon or need to be repaired. It's not under warranty anymore and I can only imagine how much it would cost. It would definitely make things tighter for me unless I got a job in town or on campus."

"Ouch. Hopefully it's just a one-time thing and not a sign of things to come." I bit my tongue before I did something I would regret. I almost offered to buy her a new laptop because I knew it would make things so much easier for her than having to worry about dealing with a laptop that wasn't working or having to find a computer on campus to use. But I couldn't, because I knew she wouldn't take it and would be offended that I offered.

"I'm sure everything will be—"

I stopped what I was doing and waited for her to say something else, but she didn't. "Iris?"

She didn't respond.

What in the actual fuck?

"Iris?" I called again as I grew more concerned.

She still didn't respond.

However, this time, I did hear some shuffling on the other end of the line, but I couldn't make it out. Someone or something was definitely near the phone, but I had no idea what.

Then I heard a voice that sounded really deep. It obviously wasn't Iris, it sounded like a man. Due to the positioning of the phone, I couldn't hear what he said. Was Iris in danger?

As if she heard the question that I'd asked myself, I finally heard Iris speak, but I couldn't make out what she was saying either. Relief flooded through me as I realized that Iris was okay.

"Iris!" I yelled, hoping that this time she heard me.

"Hey, yeah. I'm here."

"What the hell happened? Your voice was muffled, and I couldn't tell what was going on."

"I ran into someone because I zoned out while I was talking to you."

I sighed, happy that was all that happened, and she was safe. I wasn't surprised she hadn't been paying attention to where she was going. "You would do that."

It took her another couple of seconds before she replied. "Anyway, what were we talking about?"

"I don't remember," I said as I let out a yawn. "I think my panicking made me tired."

"Or you were already tired. It is kind of late."

She wasn't wrong, but I had no intention of telling her that I'd just woken up only a couple of hours ago. "True, but I'll stay on the phone with you until you get back to your room."

"Thanks. Now tell me what's new with you."

I started telling her about what was going on at Brentson, making sure to avoid anything that could hint at my alcohol usage. I'd deal with my own shit later.

10

BIANCA

About a week later, I was checking my phone as I was walking into my next class when my mouth dropped open in shock. It was as if I instinctively knew something was wrong because I could sense something was amiss before my eyes zeroed in on the problem.

Easton. Sitting in this classroom with one ankle propped up on his knee.

Easton was taking the same class as me now. He must have switched his schedule because he hadn't been in my class the week before. When he looked up and saw me, a smug grin appeared on his face. Despite my stomach dropping to my toes, I diverted my gaze and told myself to keep walking because I didn't want to give him any of my attention. I needed to make sure I picked a seat that was nowhere near his.

I was cursing out everything I could in my head as I walked to the other end of the classroom.

Once I found a desk that was empty, I sighed louder than I planned to. I dropped my bag down at my feet and slid into the chair. I opened it and took out the things I needed for this course as I tried to organize myself before today's class began.

"Something is out to get me," I muttered under my breath. What were the chances that Easton would be in my class? Brentson wasn't small by any means, so it seemed as if something was determined to make my life a living hell.

I'd done my best to avoid Easton over the last couple of years. While we'd been in the same room as one another on numerous occasions, I'd stayed away from him at all costs and had mostly succeeded. While I didn't know the exact number of words I'd spoken to him over the last two years, I was pretty sure it was less than a hundred.

"Hey, Bianca," the voice was closer than expected and my body tensed involuntarily.

I clenched and unclenched my fist that was resting on my leg before I turned my head to look at him. It was Easton, standing there with his backpack thrown over one shoulder and a smirk tugging at the corners of his mouth. "Is anyone sitting here?"

I glanced at the empty desk to my right. "Yes, I think they went to the bathroom," I lied without remorse. My voice was steady despite my heart racing at a million miles an hour. I was doing my best to not draw attention to us, but the anger I still felt toward him was making it difficult. I wasn't about to play his stupid games.

"Come on, Bianca. There's no one sitting here."

I groaned under my breath. "That doesn't mean that I want *you* to sit here."

"What if I promise not to bite?"

My eyes widened for a split-second before I caught myself. "Leave me alone, Easton," I whispered.

It was then I realized that my fingernails were digging into my leg and would more than likely leave a mark. The pain was the only thing that was helping me maintain my composure. However, it was obvious that he wasn't going to give up. I couldn't continue to pretend he wasn't there because he would only get more obnoxious. Since the time that we'd slept together, he had no issue ignoring me the same way I was ignoring him. This was a complete one-eighty, and it was clear that he was intentionally trying to press my buttons. What was also irritating was that he still had an effect on me, but there was no way I was admitting that to anyone.

"I've been here longer than you today, and there's been no one else here, Bianca."

"Then why the hell did you ask?"

"To see what you'd say," he teased. He leaned into me, and I could feel his breath tickling my ear.

"I don't want you sitting here," I replied as I tried to contain my emotions.

Easton sat down in the chair beside me, and it took everything within me not to scream.

But he only laughed, clearly enjoying being a shit stirrer. "Can't you pretend that you don't hate me for just one class, princess?" he said mockingly.

I moved my arm when his fingers brushed against it. Yet I still shivered despite myself, hating the effect he still had on me.

"Would you quit it?" I snapped, turning away from him to focus on anything else. I'd never wished so much for a class to start in my life.

"Why, when this is so much fun?"

"Seriously, can you just leave me alone?" My anger was dripping from every word. I could see the smile on his face growing wider, confirming how much he was enjoying this.

"I could, but now that I know that we share a class together, I can't resist."

I glared at him, wishing it was okay for me to slap the smile off his face.

Thankfully, my prayers were answered as Dr. Chen walked into the room. "We have a couple of minutes before we need to start, so settle down and then we'll begin."

Today we were supposed to be learning about the major schools of thought, including behaviorism, psychoanalysis, and humanism. I was excited to learn more about them, but with Easton distracting me, I wasn't sure how much I would retain.

A light breeze came through the open window closest to me and I shivered involuntarily.

"Cold?" he leaned over and whispered. "All you needed to do was ask me to keep you warm."

"Do you ever shut up?" I asked as my cheeks became warm due to anger and embarrassment. I hated how easily he could cause me to feel this way.

He muttered something under his breath that I didn't catch, and I didn't bother to ask him to repeat what he said. Dr. Chen started her lesson and I forced myself to pay extra attention to what was going on because it meant I was ignoring Easton.

I made sure to take as many notes as possible, with as much detail as I could. Not only would it help me when I was studying, but it helped me focus on ignoring Easton.

Speaking of, he tried to get my attention several times and

it made me wonder if I'd been transported back to high school. When I didn't acknowledge him, he finally turned away. While I wasn't sure what he was doing, I hoped he was paying attention to what Dr. Chen was teaching.

But I knew that was a lie.

I could feel his eyes on me, burning a hole through me. It reminded me of how I knew he was staring at me when I walked away from him in Nash's apartment. His gaze scorched my soul then. Now he was setting a blaze within me, but it wasn't driven by hurt.

Not this time.

I glanced at Easton and found him looking at me, obviously not paying attention to our lecture. It was then that I made a promise to myself.

This ended today.

I needed to stay calm right now because causing a scene wouldn't work. It would only encourage Easton to act more like a dick. No, I wouldn't give him the satisfaction of realizing he was driving me over the edge and definitely not in a good way.

I did my best to focus on what was being taught even as the tension in my stomach grew. I didn't want to have this confrontation, but if it would bring me peace in the end, it was well worth it.

I just needed to ignore him until the end of class.

Out of the corner of my eye, I could see that he was trying to get my attention, but I refused to give in.

When Dr. Chen dismissed us, I turned to Easton and asked, "Do you have a second to talk?"

"I do," he replied as he was shoving his things into his bag.

I quickly hurried to do the same because I wanted to get this over and done with. I looked up as I was zippering my bag shut and saw him leaning on the desk he'd just occupied, with his arms crossed over his chest. He was pretending like he was looking out the window, but I knew his attention was completely focused on me.

I walked away from him and toward the exit without another word. I didn't need to look behind me to know he was following because I could feel his presence. It took about a minute to find an empty classroom, but once I did, I opened the door and turned on the lights. Easton shut the door behind him and turned to face me.

The smug look on his face made me want to snap, but I took a deep breath to maintain my cool. "What do you want from me, Easton?"

"What do you mean, 'what do I want?'"

I gritted my teeth with my lips closed before I loosened my jaw. "You know exactly what I mean. We haven't had a real conversation in years, and now you want to pretend like it's cool for you to be teasing and mocking me. I won't stand for it."

"Do you think about our last conversation?"

His response caught me off guard. "Um... no." It was a lie, but he didn't have to know that.

He shrugged and crossed his arms once more. His body language screamed that he wasn't sure he wanted to talk about this topic, but his eyes shined with all the confidence anyone could muster. "I think about it often, along with what happened the night before."

I could feel something within me snap. I'd wanted to go into this with a level head, but his words made me reach my breaking point. My hands curled into fists, and it took me counting to five before I felt as if I had enough of a handle on my emotions that I could guarantee I wasn't going to hit him.

"Listen, I don't know what game you're playing, but you're not about to drag me down into your shit. You and I both said some things that day, and that was the end of it. Just because you're my brother's best friend, doesn't mean that I have to entertain any of this. Now what is it that you want?"

Easton looked down at the ground and I could see a slight smile forming on his face. It only infuriated me even more.

"I didn't expect such a response from you, especially since it's been years. I'm impressed with how you're handling yourself."

My mouth dropped open slightly, and then I threw my arms up in anger. "You know what? I don't care anymore about what you want with me. But what you're going to do, is stop harassing me, stay the hell away from me, and forget we ever spoke... or fucked."

I didn't wait to hear what his response was. I marched over to the classroom door and swung it open. Without a backward glance, I walked out of the room, daring him to follow me as I left.

I didn't stop until I made it outside to a small park that was located on campus. I looked around to double check that he hadn't followed me. When I realized he hadn't, I finally was able to calm my nerves enough to be able to think.

Did I think this was over?

Not by a long shot.

Deep down, I knew that this was only the beginning of whatever the hell he was doing. Because ever since we first met, things with him and me were never that simple.

I wished I could make it stop.

The panic. The busyness that surrounded me.

All of it. I just wanted to make it all stop.

It was later that night, after I ran into Easton in my psychology class, and I couldn't get the interaction out of my head. I took a swig from the glass of wine I had in front of me and stared off into the nothingness that was my apartment. Sure, I had all I needed here and could do anything I wanted, but staring into the abyss seemed much more attractive to me.

On the surface, I had it all. I was the mayor's daughter who never wanted for anything monetarily. My brother, best friend, and my sorority sisters loved me. My mother cared for me at times. I would love to say that my father did too, but that was a story for a different day.

I took another big gulp of the wine in front of me. It was my third glass of the night. While I knew I should stop, I didn't want to. The alcohol was helping to numb the pain I felt, and I was alright with that for now.

Tomorrow, I would deal with the consequences. After all, this was reason for a celebration, even though it looked as if right now I was doing anything but.

I'd kept my cool today, and I was proud. I didn't have a sip of alcohol throughout my whole time in the city, including at a gala I was forced to attend tonight. The urge to wash away my feelings about having to be somewhere I didn't want to be was strong, but I resisted.

But that ended as soon as I got back to my apartment. Once I was in the comfort of my own space, I took the opportunity to unwind, although by the looks of it, I probably should have stopped drinking a while ago.

I stared at the wineglass in front of me, debating with myself whether it made sense to drain the rest of the wine.

Before I could make a decision, there was a knock on my front door.

I felt my head swim, I contemplated opening the door. Who was that? Could I keep myself together enough to open the door?

I was going to ignore the person at the door because it seemed like a bad idea to answer, but then they knocked again.

With a deep sigh, I stood up and made my way to the door. When I opened it, I was met with an unexpected surprise. On the other side stood a woman from the front desk of my apartment building, holding a vase of beautiful white roses and blue hydrangeas.

"Good evening," she said with a smile. "These were delivered for you." She gestured to the vase in her hands, filled with delicate flowers.

This small gesture of kindness was sweet, but I didn't know who sent them. After thanking her, I grabbed the vase, and she closed the door once she left. It probably wasn't best for me to be attempting to carry this given how much I'd been drinking, but I made it to the kitchen counter unscathed.

I took a moment to smell the flowers, enjoying the way they tickled my nose and how wonderful they smelled. It took me a moment to find the card and once I had I almost dropped it in shock.

I'm sorry.
-E

HIS PHONE NUMBER WAS INCLUDED, and I couldn't help but roll my eyes and rip up the small card. Easton knew why I couldn't stand him since he did what he did to me. Yet he did everything in his power to insert himself into my life just to piss me off. Although I would miss Nash, the sooner they both graduated from Brentson, the fucking better.

I debated throwing out the flowers, but they were too pretty to do so. I sniffed them one more time and took the opportunity to admire them.

When my phone vibrated on the table, I was jolted out of the memories that I tried so hard to push away. I walked back to my coffee table and the text message on the screen was the last thing I expected.

> Unknown Number: B, the fun has just begun.

My mouth dropped open as I reread the text.
Who the hell was this?

11

EASTON

The smell of books filled my nose as I settled into the worn wooden chair at a table in the library. I unpacked my notebooks and textbooks before I checked the time. I ran a hand across my face when I saw that it was seven in the evening. I looked down at the items in front of me and picked up my pen.

Where the hell was Nash? We'd agreed to meet half an hour ago so we could study for our philosophy quiz, but there was no sign of him yet. With a sigh, I cracked my neck as I tapped my pen impatiently against the chipped table.

I put the pen down and picked up my phone. As I was about to mindlessly scroll, something caught my eye. My gaze landed on a bright blonde head, and it didn't take me long to realize that it was Bianca.

She was reading from a book that looked like she'd grabbed it from the library. I watched as she bit her lip, I assumed due to her trying to concentrate on the words in front of her. I hated that I couldn't take my eyes off her. I'd done my best to make her hate me and the main reason for that was because I knew what we did two years ago shouldn't go beyond that night.

The flowers that I sent were a way for me to say I was sorry, but I had a feeling it would fall on deaf ears. That was okay though because I had a backup plan that I hadn't wanted to use, but now it seemed as if I had no other choice.

A yawn fell from my lips as I turned my attention back to my notebook, choosing to focus on existentialism instead of Bianca.

But that still didn't help me figure out where Nash was. Having him here would almost guarantee that I wouldn't look in Bianca's direction because I didn't want to deal with his questions. I scrolled through my phone to get to my text messages and found nothing from Nash. I decided to send him a message.

> Me: Are we still meeting up to study?

I almost put my phone face down on the desk after I sent the message, but something caught my eye. I didn't get the notification that my message had been delivered, which was odd. I had full service where I was so the only explanation was that his phone was off. That was odd.

When I looked up again, Bianca was still sitting there, one hand in her hair and chewing on the top of her pen. I was surprised she hadn't looked up and found me staring at her. Part of me wished she would, but I already knew that the sight of me would make her rage and I'd rather not piss her off right now.

Since my phone didn't vibrate, notifying me that I had a new text message or call, I buried myself in my textbook and began taking handwritten notes for my quiz. Since it wasn't a major exam, I opted not to bring my laptop with me, choosing to go the old-fashioned route with a pen and paper.

Every so often, I would look up and stare at Bianca before I caught myself and looked back down at the work in front of me. Clearing my throat, I looked down at the pages of my book. However, no matter how hard I forced myself to focus, my attention kept wandering. The rustle of a page turning, the scratch of Bianca's pen across paper, the sound of her typing on her keyboard, the way she tucked her hair behind her ear. Any of it was enough to draw my attention to her.

I was convinced that I might have had more success studying in my apartment versus here right now, but Nash thought that the library might be a good change of scenery. Then, he had the nerve not to show up.

As I was finishing up a paragraph, I looked up and noticed that Bianca was standing. She took the opportunity to stretch and as a result, I watched as her shirt lifted slightly, showing a sliver of her stomach. It made me itch to touch it and so much more, but I knew I wasn't allowed to.

At least not yet.

After finding out that we now were taking a class together, I knew this was a sign that, although I fucked up, there was something there.

And I was determined to prove that to her, even if it took years.

By the time Bianca started packing up her things, I swore that I'd re-read the same sentence in my textbook at least ten times without comprehending a word. I couldn't help but watch Bianca put her things in her bag, double-checking to make sure she didn't leave anything behind. A couple of times, she looked over her shoulder as if she was looking for someone or something, and I couldn't help but wonder what that was all about. There was no one near her, but maybe she'd heard something I couldn't that made her suspicious.

Once she finished packing her bag, she tossed it over her shoulder and looked around the table she was sitting at one last time. As she was about to leave, one of her sorority sisters with HΣN written across her sweatshirt, stopped Bianca and began to talk to her quietly. I watched as Bianca nodded along to whatever was being said and together, they left the library, none the wiser that I'd been watching her since I arrived.

At least now I wouldn't have anything to stare at so I could get what I needed to done. Then again, since she'd left, there was also a chance I would do nothing but think about her, which wasn't helpful to me either.

I ran a hand through my hair and tried to focus on my textbook once more. That lasted only about a minute or two before I heard a commotion that forced my attention away.

There was a small bang and then almost like a flash, Nash was walking past where I was seated.

"Dude," I said, trying to get his attention. Nash looked in my direction and gave me a slight head nod before he made his way to the table. To put it mildly, he looked like a train wreck. His clothes looked disheveled. His backpack was opened with some of the contents spilling out. He was breathing slightly hard, and I knew he was in pretty good shape because we worked out together and played football on the same team. His usually neat hair was tousled, as if he'd been running his hands through it repeatedly.

"What the hell is going on with you, man?" I whispered to

not bring more attention to us in case there was someone else around.

"Nothing, everything is fine. I'm sorry I'm late." Nash placed his arms on the table as he took the seat across from me. He glanced at me before resting his head on his arms, and I wondered if he might be trying to fall asleep.

He was full of shit. I nudged him with my foot and then said, "Like hell it is. Something is obviously wrong, and I've never seen you show up anywhere this late or look like this outside of practice and game day."

Nash lifted his head and ran a hand through his hair. "I swear it's nothing."

But we both knew that was a lie. It was then that I noticed that he had bags under his eyes. "Did you get any sleep last night?"

All he did was shrug without responding, giving me an answer without saying a word. He didn't get much sleep the night before.

"If I could tell you, I would, but I can't right now."

That made the warning bells louder in my mind. Nash's attempt to evade me was half-assed. His appearance made it seem as if he'd been through hell and back, and now he couldn't talk about it?

"That's bullshit and you know it." I leaned forward, daring him to continue lying to me. "Something is obviously wrong, and if you thought I wouldn't notice it, then you must think I'm an idiot. You should have just canceled tonight so I wouldn't have seen you."

Nash stared me down, and I hoped he would start talking. Instead, he looked away and mumbled something under his breath.

"You know that you can tell me what's wrong." I kept my voice low, hoping that he would open up.

After a long moment of hesitation, Nash looked me in the eye once more. There was a haunted look in his eyes, and I wasn't sure how to feel about it.

"Easton, I'm in over my head," he said quietly. "And this is the first time in a long time I'm not sure if I'm doing the right thing."

"I'm still confused—"

Nash shook his head and said, "Never mind. Forget I said anything."

Rather than call him out on his bullshit again, I tried a different tactic. "Does it have something to do with your ex-girlfriend?"

This time, Nash glared at me because I brought her up. While I wasn't exactly clear on their whole breakup, I did know that she'd left town years ago and then, out of nowhere, transferred to Brentson this year. It was a sore subject for him, but it needed to be asked.

"This isn't the first time this has happened this year, and we are still at the beginning of the semester."

"Don't you think I know that?" Nash snapped.

I raised an eyebrow at him because his outburst was unexpected, and I didn't appreciate it. I chalked it up to the state he was currently in physically and mentally, but he didn't need to take it out on me.

"Listen, Easton. There's a shit ton of things going on, and I lost my cool."

"If this is your way of apologizing, then I accept."

That made Nash chuckle, dispersing the tension between

us, but it didn't remove the elephant in the room. "When and if I can tell you more, I will. I swear."

I nodded and then said, "I'll chill for now, but you do realize how weird this looks?"

He nodded, but seemed grateful that I was willing to back off. "So, philosophy?"

"Sure, let's get to it." After all, it's what I'd been waiting to do for at least the last forty minutes.

With a sigh, I sat up and put my head back down in my textbook again. Even with everything somewhat back to normal, I couldn't focus on the text in front of me. My thoughts were swirling with the unanswered questions that sat between us, and how and when I would find out the truth.

I cleared my throat and tried to focus on taking notes again. When I glanced up at Nash, he seemed to be doing the same, but I wasn't fully convinced that he was able to concentrate either. I hated that while the tension between us had lessened, it was still there due to all the things that had been left unsaid.

12

BIANCA

The sound of forks and knives clinking against the small appetizer plates filled the air as the people around me chatted among themselves before dinner was served. I'd only been here for twenty minutes, and I was already over it. Once you'd been to one of these things, you'd been to them all.

I found myself gravitating toward the soft candlelight illuminating from LED candles and the images they created, instead of trying to bring myself to talk to other people. While I should have been trying to make small talk like everyone else, I couldn't bring myself to do it.

I tucked a strand of hair behind my ear and ran a hand down my emerald dress. While I wouldn't mind being in a pair of sweatpants, I did have to admit that this was a beautiful dress.

"Ms. Henson."

I look up and find myself face-to-face with someone I'd seen often at these parties my parents attend. Tristan Whitmore gave me a warm smile that I refused to return. The main reason why he was here? He was in my parents social circle in part because he was slightly younger than them and he was both rich and powerful due to him being a media mogul. He owned a ton of television and radio stations and as a result, had been making his mark on several online platforms. He had no problem donating to my father's campaign even though he was a mayor of a town hours outside of New York City.

"It's nice to see you again, Mr. Whitmore," I said, lying through my teeth.

"How many times do I have to tell you to call me Tristan?"

Before I could respond I heard something that grabbed my attention.

"Ah, Bianca!"

I jumped slightly when I heard my father's voice boom from across the room. He waved me over to a small group, which included my mother. All their smiles were just as fake as his. As I approached with Tristan right behind me, I noticed Easton's parents, Oliver and Amelia Beaumont, were in the small group of people my parents were talking to. I caught myself before my face registered how I was feeling inside: shock.

"It's great to see you again, Bianca."

"Likewise, Mr. and Mrs. Beaumont." I panicked slightly because if Easton's parents were here, did that mean he was too? I'd been doing my best to avoid and ignore him despite the class we had together, and so far, it had worked. "It's always lovely to see you both."

"Thank you, dear," Amelia said, her smile soft, and I

couldn't help but wonder if it was genuine. At least during all our interactions, she treated me better than her son, and that was saying something. She looked every bit the picture of elegance in her pearl cocktail dress. "We wouldn't miss this for the world."

My heart pounded in my chest as I wondered if Easton would make an appearance tonight. I'd rarely seen him at these events, but with my brother being around here some-where, and with his newly found interest in me again, I wouldn't be surprised if he showed up. Pushing the thought out of my mind, I focused on the conversation I was having with the Beaumonts, including talking about how my semester at Brentson was going and upcoming events I would be attending with my parents.

That was until my mother spoke up.

"Is Easton joining us tonight?" my mother asked.

"Unfortunately, he wasn't able to make it," Amelia replied. "But I'm sure he'll be sad he missed you, Bianca. He mentioned that you had a class together this semester."

I felt my cheeks grow warm. I took a deep breath before I tried to play it off. "Yes, we do. Psychology."

My mind went blank when Easton's mother admitted that he'd talked to her about me. I couldn't help but wonder what he said, but I wasn't sure how or if I could get her to talk about the conversation they'd had.

Thankfully, the conversation transitioned from Easton and me to other topics. I hated that I was slightly intrigued about why he wasn't here, but I refused to ask for more infor-mation. After all, it wasn't my business, and I should just be relieved that he wasn't.

"Amelia and I just returned from a trip to Italy. The Amalfi Coast is absolutely wonderful, especially this time of year."

"Really?" I was happy to engage in this conversation because it took the heat off anything related to Easton and me, and I hadn't had the opportunity to travel to Italy yet. "What did you like most about it?"

"Oh, there were so many things we loved," Amelia said as her eyes lit up. "But I think we loved our visit to Positano the most. The beautiful water and colorful buildings cascading down the cliffs to the sea were absolutely stunning. It felt as if we were walking through a painting."

"That sounds divine," my mother added, a faraway look appearing in her eyes. "Van, we should plan a trip to Italy."

"Absolutely," my father agreed as he patted my mother on the arm.

However, I could tell that Dad's mind was elsewhere, and I was willing to bet that it was on his mayoral reelection campaign.

As we continued to discuss the Beaumonts' recent travels, I couldn't help but feel jealous. I wished that I could have the chance to travel more. I made a mental note to myself that the next opportunity I got, I was going to go somewhere I'd never been before. Maybe I could convince Iris to go with me.

"Good evening, everyone."

I turned to face the newcomer and mumbled a curse under my breath.

Diana Caldwell, the other candidate running for mayor of Brentson this election cycle, joined our conversation. I didn't know if it was my bias about her, but her smile seemed sharp and calculating. Her gaze stayed on Tristan for a little longer than necessary before it landed on me before she spoke. "I couldn't help but overhear your conversation about traveling. Have you ever considered joining one of those volunteer programs abroad? They're all the rage among young people these days, or so I've heard."

"Actually, I have," I replied cautiously, aware of Diana's ability to twist someone's words to benefit herself. I also thought it was interesting that she didn't list any of these volunteer programs by name. "It's something I want to look into, but I haven't had the opportunity to yet. I've been staying closer to home to be near my family."

"Of course," Diana agreed, but I could tell that she didn't give a shit. "Family is important, after all. And speaking of families, Oliver, Amelia, how was your trip to Italy?"

"Delightful," Mrs. Beaumont responded, though I could see the hesitance in her gaze. "The Amalfi Coast is truly stunning."

"I completely agree," Tristan added.

"Ah, yes," Diana said as her eyes narrowed slightly. "Maybe I'll have to plan a trip there myself once this election is over."

I thought it was interesting that Diana had taken over the conversation, much like she preferred to do whenever she entered the room. I glanced at my father who was quietly chatting with Mr. Beaumont, but Dad wasn't completely oblivious. I saw him glancing at Diana out of the corner of his eye. While he tried to control his emotions, I could see that her being here was annoying him.

As the conversation continued, I found myself growing

more and more uncomfortable because I could feel Diana watching me. Our conversation became more tense because it felt as if I was in a tennis match as I watched Diana attempting to show us all up and the rest of us trying to avoid confrontation. This conversation was exhausting, and I needed to get out of here. I watched as my dad and Tristan left, and Mr. Beaumont rejoined the group. I couldn't help but wish that was also me.

"Diana, it's been so long since we've seen you," my mother interjected, her voice steady and not betraying any of the thoughts running through her mind. "You simply must tell us about that new project you're spearheading. We were chatting about the revitalization of downtown earlier today weren't we, Bianca?"

I wanted to mumble bullshit under my breath, but I controlled the urge.

"Actually, Mom," I said, noticing that if I wanted to get out of this situation, I needed to make my own escape plan. "I think I left my phone in my coat. I should go grab it." I gave her a weak smile in hopes that she would get the hint that I didn't want to be involved in this discussion anymore.

"Bianca, don't worry about your phone," she insisted, her eyes flickering with concern. "Stay and chat with everyone."

"Really, Mom, I should grab it. I need to tell Easton that we need to study for our upcoming psychology exam soon and I don't want to forget again." It was a flimsy excuse and a complete lie, but if it worked, then so be it.

"Ah, Easton," Diana chimed in. "I didn't know he was taking a class in psychology. I wonder if he plans on pursuing something in the field once he graduates."

I'd had enough. "Enjoy the rest of your evening, everyone," I said, forcing a polite smile on my face as I moved away from the group. With every step I took away from them, the knot in my chest loosened. In the end, I had to thank my mom for speaking up or else I would still be there.

"Whew," I muttered under my breath. Diana's slight fascination with Easton was interesting. I wondered if it was because his parents were there or if she had an actual interest in him. For what, I had no idea. It took some shuffling, but I managed to make it over to my coat to collect my phone. The next place I wanted to go was to find a quiet room where I could take the time to recharge for a moment, because I needed it after dealing with Diana for so long.

Ignoring the feeling I was getting, I focused once again on making my way through all the guests that were standing in the hallway as I tried to put as much distance as possible between myself and the woman who threatened not only my father's political career but peace for my family.

I walked down a hallway that was less crowded and came to a door that was slightly ajar. I thought I could hang out in here, but when I heard voices on the other side of the door, I stopped and decided to eavesdrop. My mouth dropped open when I recognized both my father's voice and Nash's. What were they doing here?

"...The Chevaliers," I caught from my father, his tone laced with concern.

My heart skipped a beat, and I leaned closer as I tried to make out what was being said. The Chevaliers was a secret society that the men in my family had been a part of for generations. While I knew some things about it, for the most part, it was only from pieces of conversations that I'd been able to build a small picture of what it was. But why would Dad and Nash be discussing anything related to it here?

Nash cleared his throat and said, "I know you're worried about this, Dad, but I can handle it. This is what we agreed on me doing when I first joined, and if the opportunity presented itself."

"Can you?" my father replied sharply. "You're putting yourself at risk by doing this, Nash. Not to mention our whole family."

I couldn't help but wonder if he was actually talking about our family or if he was referring to his mayoral race.

"I can handle this, Dad. Trust me," Nash said. I could hear some irritation in his voice as he seemed to be getting annoyed with our father.

"Handle this?" There was a brief pause before my father continued, his voice softer, tinged with sadness. "I thought I had everything under control once too. And then I failed."

"No offense, but I'm not you. I have a shot at this, and I want to take it. I need to do this. Plus, I assume things are different now. We've learned from where things went wrong in the past."

"Have we?" My father sighed, and I guess he realized that he would be wasting his breath trying to convince Nash otherwise. "I hope you're right, Son. You need to be careful," my father said.

"I will, I promise," Nash replied.

This conversation between my brother and father left me with more questions than answers. What in the world were they talking about? Why was Dad so worried?

Instead of blowing my cover, I walked away, allowing Nash and Dad to continue their conversation alone.

I tried to think about anything other than what I just heard but failed. What could Nash possibly be involved in that would bring harm to our family? I wanted to help him, but it wasn't like I could just go up to Nash, tell him what I overheard, and demand that he let me help.

I strolled down the hall, my mind heavier than it had been earlier that night as I wondered what to do next.

13

BIANCA

I tapped my foot against the leg of my desk as I waited for my psychology class to end. I'd lost count of the number of times that I'd looked at the classroom door, ready to make my exit. I had to time my escape just right so I could get out of the room before the man sitting next to me.

I glanced at Easton as he leaned back in his chair. He ran a hand through his hair, causing it to fall carelessly over his forehead. I hated that it looked as if he'd just woken up after an endless night of sex.

I hated him and wished I was the reason why his hair looked like that at the same damn time.

I turned my attention back to Dr. Chen's lecture. I tried to focus on her words, but still found myself distracted. His behavior since he'd transferred into this class had done a one-eighty. Although he was still sitting next to me, he'd left me alone for the most part, but I couldn't help thinking it was only a matter of time before he made his move.

As the class dragged on, I tried to ignore Easton and it would have been pretty easy, if it hadn't been for the fact that

I was on edge. I checked the time on my phone and sighed. Only a minute to go until class would be dismissed.

"Alright, everyone, you're free to leave," Dr. Chen announced, bringing the class to an end. "Remember to read chapter five for next week."

As students began to gather their belongings and file out of the room, I'd made sure to pack my things in advance so I could leave quickly. As I reached the door, I felt a hand on my arm, stopping me in my tracks.

"Wait," Easton said, his voice was low, but I couldn't get a read on him. "Can we talk?"

"Easton, I really don't have the time, nor do I want to."

"It'll only take a few minutes."

His fingertips were warm against my skin, making me tremble slightly. It was obvious that in spite of the hatred I'd harbored for him over the last couple of years, he still could make my heart race.

I gestured for him to move to the side so that our classmates could leave the classroom and that gave me a couple of seconds to think about his question. I knew what I was going to say and that it was a mistake, yet there was a hint of desperation in his voice, which made me more curious. "Fine. Where do you want to meet?"

"Tonight at 6:30? I'll come to you."

I lost my train of thought when he said 'come' and I refrained from shaking my head in disgust. "Sure, fine."

He gave me a small nod before he walked away.

Psychology was my last class of the day, so I immediately left the building and walked over to the BMW my parents bought me as a graduation gift. I didn't drive it much, but had decided to drive to campus today, and now I was glad I did. I wanted to get back to my apartment as fast as possible.

There were a few things I needed to do just in case Easton did show up tonight. I drove home, parked my car in the parking lot, and I almost ran to my apartment. I needed to get ready for Easton's potential visit. What sucked about it was that I only had a few hours to do so. I felt foolish doing this whole thing, not knowing what we were even talking about tonight because this could be a waste of time. Yet here I was, making sure that I cleaned up the mess that had accumulated in my apartment over the past week.

While I did have a house cleaner who came in once a week to take care of things, she wouldn't be able to help me with tonight's adventure. I should have thought about that before I agreed to him coming over.

I grabbed the laundry basket from my walk-in closet and started tossing all the clothes I'd scattered around my bedroom and living room. Once that was clear, I moved on to tidying up my desk. It took me some time to put away each item into its rightful place, but eventually it looked like the perfect aesthetic you would see on social media.

The kitchen was next, and thankfully there wasn't much to tidy up. I'd ordered takeout a couple of times over the last few days so there weren't too many dishes to clean. After quickly washing those up, I decided it would be best to eat some dinner before he arrived, so I quickly warmed up a leftover pasta dish and gathered some vegetables I could chop up and turn into a quick salad.

I chopped and washed all the produce—a tomato, a cucumber, red onion, and carrots—and put them on top of some mixed greens. I added feta cheese and a vinaigrette to the salad, and I was done.

As I sat down to eat, I allowed my mind to wander back to what this could be about. Why did he want to talk with me alone? Was this some sort of twisted game he was playing? I shook my head, convincing myself I was overthinking things. It was just a conversation, nothing more.

While I tried to enjoy the meal, I couldn't, because I couldn't get my mind off Easton. I felt uneasy, and I couldn't exactly explain why.

After I finished eating, I decided to take a shower. I wanted to feel refreshed and confident for whatever was going to happen tonight. As I stood under the hot water, I focused on relaxing instead of the other shit going on in my life and it seemed to help.

But as I rinsed off the soap, I knew that I had to find out. We needed to find a way to deal with each other because he was Nash's friend, and our families were friends. Maybe it was time to bury the hatchet and move on from where we'd been over the last couple of years.

I got dressed in my usual attire, which consisted of yoga pants and a t-shirt with a sweatshirt thrown on top. I didn't want to give Easton the wrong idea about my expectations, whatever this talk was supposed to be about. I added some light makeup to my face, but not enough to make it look as if I put in a lot of effort.

When I put down my lip balm, I got a phone call from the front desk. I checked my phone and saw that the time was 6:29 p.m. If this was Easton, then he was right on time.

"Hello, this is Bianca."

"Hi, Ms. Henson. Easton Beaumont is here to see you, but he's not on the list of people that are allowed to come up."

"You can let him up. Thank you."

I hung up the phone and was left in silence. In a matter of minutes, Easton would be in my apartment for who knew what, and I felt as if I was being dragged in front of a crowd completely naked. The last time we'd been alone, he'd told me I'd been nothing more than a quick fuck.

I strolled into the living area and sat down on the couch as I waited for him to come upstairs. A few minutes later, there was a knock on the door. I took my time walking over to it, and I looked out the peephole, confirming it was Easton. With a deep breath, I turned the lock and then the doorknob.

"Hey, Bianca," Easton said smoothly.

I hated how good he looked.

He was in a black t-shirt, dark denim pants and a leather jacket. His entire demeanor was calm, cool, and casual as he leaned against my doorframe, and I was the exact opposite and wasn't completely sure if I was in the midst of a panic attack.

"Come in."

Easton didn't waste any time coming inside, and I closed the door behind him. My manners and my mom's gift for hosting people at her home must have been passed down to me because the next thing out of my mouth was, "Can I get you something to drink or eat?"

Easton shook his head. "No thanks. I won't be staying for long."

That was a relief, but it still left me with plenty of questions.

I led Easton toward my living room and said, "Have a seat wherever you'd like."

Once he sat down on the far end of my couch, I decided to sit down on the cushion closest to me, giving us ample space from one another.

"So, what is this all about?"

Easton turned his head so that he could look me right in the eye. "Well, I want something from you, and you need something from me."

The laughter that came out of my mouth was anything but humorous. "I doubt that I need anything from you, but I'll bite. What is it that you want from me?"

Easton's gaze turned to look out my window, as if he had a sudden fascination with watching the sun set. I waited for him to continue, but I already knew I wasn't going to like the words that were going to come out of his mouth.

"I want you," he finally said.

My mouth dropped open, and I couldn't tell what was affecting me more, my shock or my disgust with him. "Do you have a concussion from football?"

That made him chuckle. "Nope, I'm completely fine."

"Easton," I warned, narrowing my eyes as I stood up to show him to the door. "I don't want anything to do with you, as I've made it obvious the last two years. Just leave me alone and you can start doing that by leaving now."

He raised his hands defensively and I rolled my eyes. "Hear me out." Easton paused, and when the look in his eyes turned wicked, I knew I was in trouble.

"Unless," he continued in a low voice, "you'd rather I go to your parents and talk to them about your little. . . drinking problem."

"What are you talking about?" I stuttered, attempting to pretend I had no idea what he was talking about. I failed.

My heart stopped as he pulled out his phone and showed me a photo. It was clearly a picture of me doing a body shot off Taylor. He flicked his thumb over the screen and I saw myself drinking while dancing on a bar top. My body involuntarily began to shake. So, he had been there the night I thought I saw him.

"Come on, Bianca," he drawled. "There's plenty more where that came from."

I wanted to smack the smug look off his face. "This is a swift jump from sending me flowers as an apology."

He ran a hand through his hair, but this time it looked anything but innocent. "It didn't work, so it was time to try something else. Let's not play games here. I know all about your little escapades with alcohol, and what you've been doing when you're wasted. If you don't want your parents—or better yet, the local media—finding out, then I suggest you reconsider my offer."

"You've got to be shitting me! Is this seriously your attempt at blackmailing me into sleeping with you?"

"You call it blackmail; I call it ensuring that I get what I want."

"You're a miserable son of a bitch."

"That is an accurate description."

He knew that he had me where he wanted me. There was no way I wanted any of this to get out because I honestly didn't know what would be worse: the media reporting on it, or having my parents probably disown me for ruining my father's chances at reelection because the general public would think he needed to spend more time disciplining me.

"What I don't understand is what you want from me. There's no shortage of people on this campus that want to fuck you, so what the hell do you want from me?"

Easton stood up, causing me to look up at him. "I don't want to fuck anyone else. I want you, princess."

His boldness made me take a step back, putting some much-needed distance between us. I'd spent the last few hours going over and over in my head possibilities for what he wanted with me, and him blackmailing me into sex had not been on the list. And I couldn't believe how casually he had just laid it out on the line. This whole incident felt like one big case of whiplash, with no signs of stopping.

"I'll be somewhat nice and give you a bit of time to think things over."

"You call that being nice?"

Easton scoffed. "I mean, I don't need to do that." He paused for a moment at the door before he opened it. "I'll be seeing you around, Bianca."

"Wait."

Easton stopped and turned to look back at me, his eyes reading every inch of my face.

"Why now? You had the opportunity to have this discussion with me two years ago, and you made me feel like shit."

"There were some things that happened a couple of years ago, which stopped me from making a move on you then. Now, I have no issue taking what I want, by any means necessary. Good night, Bianca."

With that, he walked out of my apartment, leaving me reeling from our encounter.

14

EASTON

I glanced at the sun hanging low in the sky as it cast a golden glow over Brentson University's football field. I stood beside Nash, slightly out of breath as the sweat felt like it was coming out of every pore. Our teammates were spread out across the grass, running drills and plays to prepare for our next game.

"Man, I can't believe we are already halfway through the season," Nash said, wiping his face with the back of his hand. "Feels like it just started."

"It really does," I replied, glancing at him out of the corner of my eye. Things had gotten better since the last time I saw him. It almost looked as if things were back to normal with him, but there was still that feeling in the back of my mind since we met up to study in the library.

"Alright, listen up!" Coach Klein yelled, his whistle swinging from a lanyard around his neck. "One more time!"

I could feel the excitement pouring off everyone after the announcement. Although adrenaline was flowing through our veins from practice, I was willing to bet all of us were tired and ready to crash.

We got into position and the ball snapped. With my heart pounding in my chest, I took off, running down the field. I tracked the ball and saw the instant Nash hurled it in my direction.

I stretched out my arms in an effort to catch the football. For a split-second, everything blurred around me. Then, with a resounding smack, the ball collided with my palms, and I brought it into my chest, sprinting the final few yards into the end zone. I could hear the cheers and shouts converging on me as I spiked the ball triumphantly, since I couldn't do that in a real game.

I walked over to Nash and found him sitting on the ground. He looked exhausted, but I didn't blame him because I felt the same. He slapped my helmet and said, "That was a hell of a catch."

"Thanks, dude." I waited a beat and then said, "Done?"

"Yeah, man. I'm done," he said as he nodded.

I waited until he got up to toss him the football.

"Did that help you get the stick out you've had up your ass for the last week?" I was being a bit harsh, I admitted, but it was the truth. Every time I saw him lately, he seemed to be in a bad mood.

Nash shoved me hard and all I did was chuckle. Then he said, "I feel better."

"Better enough to text Raven? Maybe she can pull the stick out."

Raven was his ex-girlfriend that he'd never gotten over, and now that she was back in town, things had suddenly become... interesting between the two of them.

"You don't ever shut up, do you?"

I shrugged. "You should know by now that I don't."

I glanced away and saw that Coach Klein raised his whistle to his lips and blew. "Great job, everyone," he called out. "That's it for today!"

The shrilling sound of the whistle echoed through the air once again, signaling the end of practice. As we left, Nash cleared his throat, drawing my attention to him. The excitement that was once on his face was long gone and I couldn't help but wonder what had removed it.

"Are you alright?" I asked.

"Yeah, I am. There was something I wanted to tell you."

On one hand, I wondered briefly if Bianca had told Nash about the encounter that she and I had, but that idea quickly flew out the window. There was no way she had, because without a doubt, Nash would have come and found me, ready to snap my neck instead of congratulating me on a sweet catch.

"Of course," I replied, waiting for him to continue.

"There's something I've been meaning to tell you related to that whole library incident." Nash trailed off as he looked around, probably trying to see if there was anyone around us.

"Is there something you need me to do?"

Nash shook his head. "It isn't anything like that. This is something I've been tasked with doing, and while it is something I've been struggling with and don't completely know how to handle, it's also not something I can ask for help on."

This didn't sound related to school at all. Brentson University thrived on letting students have access to a number of resources to help them with their studies. Plus, the Hensons had enough money to make sure that either Nash got the help he needed, or they could pay off the college to pass him, so I doubted this had anything to do with school.

"This all sounds very vague. What's going on?"

"There are some things that I'm having to do for an organization I'm a part of, which have been tedious to say the least. That's where I was right before I was supposed to meet up with you to study for philosophy."

I nodded my head slowly as I tried to process what he was telling me. "That is still super vague, but kind of explains what has been going on with you."

"I know, but I wanted to tell you so that you kind of got the gist of what's been happening."

I remained quiet as I thought about what he said and what this organization might be. Here he was trying to open up to me, while I was keeping a huge secret from him. I was struggling with keeping what was going with Bianca from him. She hadn't responded to my offer yet and I was willing to give her time... for now.

"Easton."

"What?" I said, startled that Nash called my name. How long had he been calling me?

"Is everything alright with you? You've seemed distracted as well."

"Yeah, I'm fine." The lie came so easily from my lips that I could have almost convinced myself that I wasn't lying.

As we continued walking toward the locker room, I struggled with my own internal battle about the secrets I was keeping from him. Should I tell Nash about what was going on between Bianca and me? Should I mention that the basis of our friendship is a complete lie? A part of me wanted to reveal the lies that were just beneath the foundation of our friendship. But I knew it was best to keep my mouth shut because now was definitely not the right time.

"Are you sure? Whatever's going on with you, I'm here to help."

"Yeah, I swear, I'm fine. And the same goes for you."

Nash opened the door to the locker room, and we walked to get our things. As I was gathering my stuff, Nash turned to me and said, "Let's go get some food."

I thought about the things I needed to do. A shower was still on top of the list, but I was also starving, so I said, "Why not? We need to eat."

"Is that the only reason you're hanging out with me?"

That forced a laugh out of me. "That's totally the reason."

There were many reasons why I'd originally become friends with Nash, but eating dinner with him wasn't one of them.

Nash and I got ready and left campus to get some food at a local fast-food restaurant. Once we'd ordered and received our food, we found a booth to eat at and didn't speak while we stuffed food into our mouths.

As I grabbed a napkin to wipe my mouth, I said, "So how are things with Raven?"

I watched Nash's face to see if his expression would give anything away, but it didn't. "Things are progressing the way that they should be. We've had so many parties to attend over the last few weeks, including one that my parents threw. Speaking of that party, I brought her as my date."

I cleared my throat before I said, "I know that didn't go well."

"You're damn right it didn't, but it was well worth the drama it caused."

Nash had a habit of trying to piss his parents off, and I could only imagine what they thought when Raven walked in as his date. His mentioning a dinner party at his parents' home reminded me of Bianca and I hated it. I'd done my damnedest to get her off my mind since the last time I thought about her, and now I was thinking about her again. I wasn't ever going to stop at this point.

Our small talk continued until we finished our meal and then we went our separate ways. I headed back to my apartment, showered, and lounged in front of my television until I could convince myself that I needed to do the homework I had due for tomorrow. At least I only had one class to worry about so it wouldn't be too bad.

Once my assignment was complete, I got into bed and had a dreamless sleep.

THE NEXT AFTERNOON, I was busy working out, enjoying the feel of my limbs burning as I lifted weights. Since I had only one class today, working out on days like today meant that I had more time to dedicate to it. Once I was done with my last bicep curl, I grabbed my things and took the elevator back to my apartment.

I had just settled on my couch when my phone rang.

"Yo," I said when I answered the call.

"Are you busy?"

"Nah. I'm done with my classes for today. Why? What do you need?"

"I need you to stop by my place and then head to Raven's.

I'll send you a list of things to grab and drive it over here to me."

I sat up from where I was laying on my couch and asked, "Wait, why? Where the hell are you?"

"I'll send you the address, and then when you get here, I'll give you further directions."

"I'm going to need more information than that and you know it. What the hell is going on?"

"Look, I won't be on campus for a few days, and I need some things from my apartment because I didn't have time to grab them before I left," Nash said.

"Why does this sound like a secret ops mission?" The question sounded ridiculous coming out of my mouth, but I was only half-joking.

"Can you do it or not?"

His comment was abrasive and took me by surprise. "Yes. Text me the address and what you need, and I'll swing by both of your homes and get it."

"Thanks."

"But I also want to know what is going on."

"Fine. We'll discuss it when you get here."

Before I could say anything else, he hung up on me. What the fuck was that all about?

He didn't tell me when he needed me to be at this mysterious address. So, without a second thought, I left my apartment and headed over to Raven's place before going to Nash's.

15

BIANCA

I paced back and forth in my apartment as I tried to clear my thoughts. Something hadn't been sitting right with me for days and I needed to think things through. The best way for me to do that apparently, was wearing a hole in my carpet due to the number of times I'd walked the same path.

After overhearing my Dad and Nash talking, I couldn't shake the feeling that something was off with Nash. He had been acting strange for a while now and hadn't answered his phone when I called him last night either. He was more distant than usual and while I wanted to give him space to figure out whatever it was that was going on in his life, I was worried about him.

"Okay, enough is enough," I muttered under my breath. I grabbed my phone, found Nash's number, and called him. The phone rang and rang, but Nash didn't answer. I waited for him to text me back, at least letting me know he saw my call, but he didn't, deepening my worry.

There was a chance he had class, I supposed, but if I remembered correctly, today wasn't a practice day.

Still, I had a bad feeling, and I couldn't just keep pacing in my apartment and doing nothing. I could call my parents and have them meet me at Nash's place, but I preferred to do this alone in case I was overreacting.

I grabbed my jacket and a purse that would contain everything I needed and headed out the door. I was going to get to the bottom of this if it was the last thing I did.

The cool autumn air hit me as I stepped outside, but I barely felt it. The only thing that mattered was getting over to Nash's place and finding out what was up with him. I walked down the street because thankfully, it was only a couple of blocks away from mine.

As I approached Nash's apartment building it began to rain.

"Damn it," I said, wishing I would have driven instead. My heart began to race because I didn't know what I would find when I got there. What if he was in some kind of trouble? The fact that the last thing I heard my father and Nash discussing was the Chevaliers did little to calm me down. Who knew what type of activities they were up to.

I inhaled a long, deep breath in order to steady myself as I pushed open the heavy glass doors, making my way to the elevator.

I played with the key to Nash's apartment as I rode up to his floor. The ride felt painfully slow, each ding of the passing floors irritated me because it sounded like a countdown to something ominous. When the elevator stopped on his floor, I tapped my foot as I waited for the doors to open and once they did, I hurried down the hallway until I reached his apartment.

I swallowed hard as I knocked on the door. When I didn't hear anything in response, I unlocked the front door and stepped inside.

"Hello," I said, and paused to see if I heard anyone. "Nash?"

"It's me, Bianca. Are you here?" But I didn't get a response.

Thankfully, it was still light outside, making it easy to see the living area. Nothing was disturbed. I didn't see Nash's bookbag, laptop, or keys, any of which would have been tell-tale signs that he was home.

But then I heard something.

It sounded like... running water? My breath caught in my throat as I strained to listen, trying to pinpoint the source of the sound.

"Hello?" I tried again, louder this time. The noise persisted, and my concern for Nash reached an all-time high. This wasn't fucking normal.

I looked around to see if I could find a weapon and walked over to get one of the large chef knives my mother insisted on buying when we moved into our apartments. It would definitely come in handy now.

I walked back into the hallway and was able to determine that the sound of water was coming from either the master or guest bathroom. Maybe Nash had decided to shower?

But then, his things not being in the living area didn't make sense.

"Stay calm, Bianca," I told myself. "Nothing weird is going on here. You can do this."

I made my way down the hallway, the sound of running

water growing clearer as I moved forward. Once I stood in front of the doors that would lead to the bedrooms in the apartment, it became apparent the noise was coming from the guest bathroom. I walked into the guestroom and found a bag on the floor near the guest bathroom door. The gym bag was unfamiliar and didn't look anything like Nash's.

"Hello?" I called out hesitantly as my grip tightened on the knife handle. As I reached for the guest bathroom doorknob, my heart thundered in my chest. The metal was stone cold against my skin, sending shivers up my spine. I knocked on this door as well and didn't get a response. It was possible that whoever it was couldn't hear me over the running water. With a deep breath, I turned the knob and pushed the door open.

The sound of water splashing echoed off the tiled walls, and I felt guilty about walking in on someone when they were showering, but whoever this was they had no business being here. Everything about this situation felt wrong, yet I couldn't tear myself away. Nash's absence did nothing but bother me, and the presence of this stranger's things only served to fan the flames of my concern.

But what I witnessed shifted my attention in a completely different direction.

The amount of steam coming from the shower and the frosty shower doors made it hard to make out the details of what I was seeing, but it was, without a doubt, a man with a very muscular back. While keeping my eye on the figure in the shower, I saw a cellphone sitting on the bathroom coun-tertop and I grabbed it. When I pressed one of the buttons on the side, the screen illuminated, allowing me to see the background image on the phone. Imagine my surprise when I saw Easton's jersey appear on the screen.

I gasped louder than intended when I realized who was taking a shower in my brother's apartment.

Easton.

I tried to back away slowly from the scene that was unfolding in front of me, but suddenly Easton turned the water off. The silence that surrounded us with the water turned off made it impossible for me to sneak out.

I still had no idea where Nash was and why Easton was taking a shower here. I stared down at the knife in my hand and realized that it was probably unnecessary for me to be holding it anymore. Instead, I placed the knife down on the counter, hitting Easton's phone and making a loud noise.

My eyes widened as I watched Easton freeze briefly before yanking the shower door open. He was naked as the day he was born and looking as if he might attack me. The angry look on his face only lasted for a minute before a smug look replaced it.

"Why didn't you just join me?"

I rolled my eyes. "Excuse me?"

"In the shower. You could have just joined me. Did you want to see if my cock was still as big as you remembered it?" He used his hand to push back his hair that was stuck to his forehead.

"Can you stop thinking with your dick for a moment?"

"Not when you're staring at it like you want me to bend you over the counter and fuck you with it."

The blush in my cheeks had nothing to do with the hot shower that Easton had been taking.

"Can you at least wrap a towel around your waist?"

"No. You barged in when I was showering, and I'm feeling rather comfortable being naked in the bathroom."

I took another deep breath to stop myself from snapping at him. Arguing with him wouldn't do anything but waste more time. "Where's Nash?"

"He's not here," Easton said. The water on his chest moved toward his waist, leaving a trail I couldn't help but follow with my eyes. He was trying to distract me and was doing a very good job of it.

"Where did he go?"

"I'm not sure."

"What do you mean you're not sure?"

"Look, Bianca," Easton sighed as his entire demeanor changed. He reached for a towel, and as he was wrapping it around his waist, he said, "I don't know all the details. The only thing he said was that he wanted me to gather some things for him from his apartment. He also wanted me to grab stuff from Raven's as well."

"Some things?" I repeated, not sure that I believed him. "You have to know more than that."

"Let's talk after I get some clothes on."

Easton's seriousness put me on edge, increasing my fear that something had happened to Nash. But I could at least wait for Easton to put on clothes.

Without another word, I stumbled out of the guest bathroom and slammed the door behind me. My face burned with a mixture of anger and embarrassment from not having answers about my brother and from watching his best friend shower.

I leaned against the hallway wall, trying to calm myself

down. Everything around me felt as if it was one big, jumbled mess that I wasn't sure I could untangle.

"Get it together, Bianca," I muttered under my breath, "None of this is about you."

Seeing Easton naked in the shower stirred up feelings within me that I had been trying to suppress due to how much of an asshole he was and how he treated me. Not to mention the shitty offer he'd given me days ago. Now I was sitting here fantasizing about him, when I should have been worried about my brother.

I walked away from the wall and into the living room. As I waited for him to finish, I couldn't help but be annoyed that my brother had decided to trust Easton and not me. Not that he couldn't have told Easton in addition to me, but after all we'd been through, why hadn't he filled me in on what was going on? Did he trust Easton more than me? Was it because I was his kid sister?

But as the minutes ticked by and Easton still hadn't come out, doubts began to creep into my mind. Maybe Nash didn't trust me.

"Fuck, why does everything have to be so complicated?"

"Because life's never simple, princess," Easton's voice drawled from behind me, causing me to jump in surprise. He was calmly standing there, his wet hair slicked back from his forehead. He was holding his gym bag and a black duffel bag.

"Easton..." I whispered, swallowing the lump in my throat. The tension between us was at an all-time high, and I wasn't sure how to feel. What I did wonder was whether he was feeling it too. "Is Nash okay?"

"As far as I know, yes."

"Then tell me what's going on with him."

"I don't know much. All I know is that he sent me a list of things he wanted me to grab from here and from Raven's and bring to an address he sent me."

He dropped the bag, and I looked through it, not seeing anything too weird. Then an idea popped into my mind.

"What was the address he gave you?"

Easton pulled out his phone and showed me the address. I gasped and read the address over twice.

"I know where that is, and I'm going with you."

16

BIANCA

"You shouldn't be here. You know that right?"

I glared at Easton as he drove us away from Brentson in the rain. "I have every right to be here now that I know you're heading up to the cabin that my grandfather gifted Nash and me."

"Have it your way."

Instead of trying to find a response to his comment, I stared out the window as I watched the trees go by. Nothing about this made sense, and I would only get the answers I wanted by going to the cabin. That is, until it hit me.

"Why would Raven and Nash be at the cabin together?"

"I'm not sure. I don't know much about her other than she just showed up at the start of the school year."

"Well, their breakup was pretty tragic in a way. Do you remember the evening that you and I met?"

"I remember it well."

I could feel his stare on me briefly, and I both hated and loved it. Reminiscing about that day wouldn't get me anywhere. I wanted to avoid the way that his words made me feel, so I shoved them to the side. "He left my parents' house and went to see Raven."

"What does that have to do anything?"

"You didn't let me finish. The next day, when he tried to talk to her, she didn't answer her phone. So, he stopped by her house, and she wasn't there. She had just vanished. Then, all of a sudden, she appears in Brentson two years later." I paused as I debated telling Easton my thoughts about the current situation. "I think Nash kidnapped her."

Easton's gaze flickered to me in an instant. "That's a big conclusion to jump to, Bianca."

"There's no way Raven would have gone anywhere with Nash willingly. Hell, if you would have asked me yesterday, I would have told you there was no way Nash would have gone anywhere with Raven either."

"Bianca, that's ridiculous. Why would he kidnap her?"

"I have no clue, but that's what I'm leaning toward more than any other explanation."

Easton shook his head and sighed. "You're grasping at straws here. There has to be another explanation."

"Okay, then what is it?" I challenged him, ready to listen to whatever theory he had in mind. I had no problem listening to what he wanted to say even though I believed I was right.

He paused for a moment before finally responding. "Maybe Nash wanted her help with something. Or maybe they were heading up to the cabin to work on a project or something else like that."

I rolled my eyes at Easton's suggestions. It sounded plausible if it was anyone else, but I still wasn't convinced. "First off, as far as I know, they don't have any classes together. Second, even if that was true, why would he go away with her in such an abrupt manner? That doesn't sound like Nash at all," I said as we continued down the road that would eventually lead us to my grandfather's cabin.

"Maybe he wanted to surprise her," Easton suggested.

I scoffed at this idea. "They don't like each other. Why would he surprise her with a trip to the cabin? That doesn't even make sense." I shook my head, still not convinced Raven had gone willingly with Nash. I just couldn't shake the feeling something wasn't right. And it hurt that I ventured to think that my brother would do such a thing.

Easton didn't add anything, and we continued on in silence for the rest of the ride, but I could tell he was thinking about what I had said. He clearly didn't want to believe my theory either, but I knew deep down that it was true.

Easton sighed again. "Well, why don't we just wait and see what's going on when we get up there," he said.

I nodded silently as I looked out the window at the trees passing by, feeling more anxious than ever before. What was Nash up to? Was Raven in danger? I had so many questions that I desperately needed answered, and all of this was giving me a massive headache.

"I know something else we can talk about."

Part of me wanted to ignore him, but that would make this car ride even less pleasant. "What is it that you want to talk about?"

"The offer I made you."

"How about we don't."

"What? You don't want to talk about how I'll be able to fuck you anytime I want? You're just denying the inevitable at this point."

"And all of this in exchange for you keeping silent about my drinking? Blackmail looks so good on you."

"As I said before, I do what I need to do to get what I want."

I laughed sarcastically because he just *had* to bring this up. "Why do I think this is my brother's philosophy as well?"

"It would explain why we're friends."

I rolled my eyes. "There's nothing really to discuss, because I haven't given you an answer."

"Bianca, I've been very patient with you."

I scoffed and slightly changed the subject back to the person of the hour. "Does Nash know you're doing this?"

I watched as his grip tightened on the steering wheel, telling me that I struck a nerve. "No, he doesn't. Plus, in a way, I'm trying to do the right thing here."

"Oh really? Please share how you being able to fuck me whenever you want because you're blackmailing me is the right thing in this scenario."

"We both know that I want to fuck you. And we also both know you've been partying hard since you got to Brentson and doing your best to hide it from your family. We're not talking the occasional sip of alcohol here and there. It's getting black out drunk on weekends and sometimes during the week. It's only a matter of time before someone at one of these parties doesn't protect you. Then the news comes out about your drinking anyway. Hell, what I was able to collect was easy enough."

He paused briefly, giving me the opportunity to digest what he was saying. I hated that he was absolutely right.

"Your parents will never forgive you if this ruins your father's reelection chances. All in all, I'm just the one who is blackmailing you first, because it was only a matter of time before it happened. This isn't some elaborate scheme just so I can get what I want from you... well, not entirely anyway. It's also about the fact you need help in controlling your drinking and making sure it doesn't get worse."

His whole monologue felt like he'd taken the knife that I was walking with through Nash's apartment earlier and stabbed me in the heart. He'd hit on so many key points that I'd thought about myself regarding my drinking, but never dared to focus on for long. Things had slowed down a bit in public, but he wasn't aware about how much I was drinking in private.

"So let me make sure I'm understanding this correctly. If I have sex with you when you want, you won't talk about my drinking problems with my family. If I don't, you'll send them all the evidence you've gathered. And somehow, this is going to stop me from drinking so much?"

"It'll make you more aware of the consequences of your actions when it comes to drinking so much."

"But what if this makes me drink even more?"

"Then we'll have to take more drastic measures."

This was ridiculous. "Most people would recommend going to a therapist or another professional that can help you with alcoholism."

Easton shrugged. "I'm trying my way first. Do I have to put a deadline on this? If you don't give me an answer, I'll have no choice but to talk to your parents."

I wanted to slam my hands down on the dashboard, but that might not be the smartest thing I'd ever done. "You do have a choice. You don't have to tell them a thing!"

Easton was silent and I wondered if he was thinking

about what I said. Maybe there was a chance that he would change his mind. "I'm giving you one more day before I want your answer. And arguing with me will cause that timeframe to decrease significantly."

I went back to ignoring him, choosing to look out the window instead of at him. I was pissed that he would put me in this predicament. Then again, it was my fault for giving him the opportunity to do it.

I was so screwed.

But I couldn't think about that now. What mattered right now was getting to Nash and finding out what was going on.

As we drove toward the cabin, the landscape began to change. Gone were the streetlights and in their place were tall pines along this narrow road. The sky above us was gray and continued to grace us with rain.

The closer we got to the cabin, the more isolated we became. I was pretty sure we were on the brink of losing our cell service. The occasional cabin or lodge we passed here and there soon became blips in the miles of untouched wilderness that we passed. I couldn't help but wonder what we would find when we reached our destination.

Easton slowed down as the GPS told us we were only four minutes from our destination. Even if the GPS hadn't confirmed it, I knew we were almost there when we drove past the larger cabin that my family also owned. We were coming up on the moment of truth, and I wasn't sure if I could handle it. "You need to go down that road," I said as I pointed out the windshield.

Easton nodded and took my direction unquestioningly, which on some level, I was surprised by.

When we pulled up in front of the smaller cabin and

Easton parked, I looked down and noticed my hand was shaking.

Easton stepped out of the car and came around and opened the door for me. After I stepped out, I watched as he went to the trunk of his SUV and pulled out the black duffel bag that had Raven and Nash's things in it.

The air seemed to be chillier than when we left Brentson. The silence that surrounded us was deafening. It made every step and breath we took seem louder than it actually was. As we approached the cabin door, I felt my heart pounding in my chest. Would we find Nash and Raven inside?

When we reached the door, I looked at Easton, who was staring back at me. He didn't say a word before he knocked on the cabin's front door.

17

EASTON

I glanced at Bianca as I waited for Nash or Raven to open the door. It only took a moment for the door to open, and I was face to face with Nash.

And to say he looked worse for wear was putting it mildly. I glanced over his shoulder at the brunette behind Nash. Obviously, this was Raven and, despite this being the first time I'd seen her, it was fair to say she wasn't looking much better than Nash at this point, and I wanted to ask what was going on. All of that went out the window when Nash spoke first.

"Bianca? What the fuck are you doing here?" Nash asked her as he glanced at me.

"I wanted to talk to you, so I went to your apartment. I was there to ask you about what happened with Mom and Dad after the party at our house, but you weren't home. Then this asshole walked through the door and told me that he was going to see you, so I made him bring me along. He wouldn't tell me where we were going, but I pieced it together once I recognized the roads we were taking."

That wasn't the way things had unfolded, but Nash didn't need to know that.

Bianca stopped talking and suddenly her eyes settled on Raven. They then drifted between the two of them as I watched her try to put together this mystery that was unfolding in front of us. Bianca walked over to Raven and gave her a small hug before returning to stand near Nash. The whole thing confused me slightly, but I was willing to watch from the sidelines for now to see what would happen.

"It makes sense why Nash is here because we co-own this place, but why are you? And what happened to you? There's so many scratches and bruises... Sorry, I'm being rude, and I apologize for being offensive," Bianca said while looking at Raven.

Before anyone else could speak or move, I pushed my way into the cabin, which was growing smaller by the second with the number of people that were in it. I placed the duffel bag at Nash's feet before taking a step back.

"Next time, give me a warning if I'm going to have to babysit your sister for a couple of hours."

Bianca turned and glared at me, but I ignored her. My goal was to keep any suspicion about why Bianca was with me and about us low.

I took a step forward and introduced myself to Raven. "By the way, I'm Easton, this fucker's best friend."

"Nice to meet you. My name is Raven," she said in return.

We shook hands before taking a step back from one another.

Bianca cleared her throat, drawing our eyes back to her as she refocused her attention on us. She side-eyed me before she turned to Raven and repeated her question again.

"I'm here because your brother—"

"Wants to keep you safe," Nash said, finishing her sentence.

Raven glared at him, and it was easy to tell that she didn't appreciate him answering for her. "I can speak for myself, thank you very much."

Bianca's mouth dropped open, and I studied Nash because I was trying to figure out if he was telling the truth or not. There's no way this was true.

"Safe from what?" Bianca questioned.

"Last night, Raven was almost kidnapped," Nash responded while he looked at Raven.

"What do you mean almost kidnapped?" I asked.

"Raven was almost kidnapped, but I stopped it from happening." Nash didn't elaborate anymore and there were still so many questions that I had. I was certain Bianca felt the same.

"And why aren't we going to the police about this?" Bianca followed up with.

"It's complicated and would only cause more confusion if the police were brought in. So, we are staying here until further notice." Nash glanced at me and said, "Were you able to find everything I asked for?"

"I was," I replied.

"Perfect. Would you both like to stay for dinner?"

Bianca smiled as her eyes darted between Nash and Raven and then she said, "We would love to."

As soon as Nash asked, I knew Bianca was going to answer for the both of us. I couldn't let her get away without me giving her a hard time. "Well, the princess has spoken, so it looks like we will be staying."

Bianca turned and glared at me once more. It was something I was quickly growing used to.

We sat down at the dining room table. Nash went into the kitchen to grab what I assumed was food. Something had smelled delicious when we walked through the door, and I couldn't wait to see what it was.

Raven cleared her throat and said, "Bianca, can we move Nash's stuff to the other end of the table so that you and I can chat? It's been so long since we've talked."

Bianca raised an eyebrow at Raven as I stood up and did as Raven asked. Bianca sat down in the chair that was once occupied by Nash, and I watched as the two women in the room smiled at each other.

When Nash walked back into the dining room, his eyes darted between Raven and Bianca. He gave Raven a small nod, and I couldn't help but wonder what he was thinking.

Nash set a plate in front of me and then said, "I have one more favor to ask."

"What's that? And thanks, man," I said.

Nash nodded. "I want to borrow your SUV while we're here."

My eyes widened, and I thought they were going to pop out of my skull. "You want to do what?"

"To ease the burden for you, I'll let you have the Jag until I'm back on campus."

I thought about it for a split second before saying, "Hell yes!"

While my SUV had cost a pretty penny, it wasn't as new as Nash's Jaguar. I'd eyed the car many times in the past as I tried to decide what my next car would be, but I hadn't settled on anything yet. Maybe this would help me reach that decision.

"Well, since that is taken care of, let's eat."

Bianca and I dug into our food wholeheartedly. I couldn't help but notice that Raven didn't eat the rest of the food on her plate. I wondered why.

Raven looked up and said, "I'm done eating, so I'm going to put my dishes in the sink. Can I take anything else?"

Everyone else at the table shook their heads so she picked up her glass and plate and walked into the kitchen. A couple of minutes later, Nash went into the kitchen, leaving Bianca and me alone.

When I heard a loud commotion, I asked, "Everything all right in there?"

"Everything is perfect," Nash called from the kitchen.

Bianca and I watched as Nash escorted Raven back into the room. She pushed his arm out of the way before she took her seat.

Nash, Bianca, and I started talking about school, while Raven remained quiet. Bianca must have noticed it too, because she brought up the danger that surrounded Raven and then asked, "Is there anything I can do to help?"

Raven shook her head and then said, "Could you take me back to campus?"

Bianca tilted her head, and out of the corner of my eye, I watched as Nash shifted in his seat. He didn't seem comfortable with this idea, and I found that interesting.

"If there's someone trying to kidnap you, it would make more sense for you to stay somewhere where no one would expect to find you," Bianca replied.

"I don't feel comfortable being here," Raven tossed back, and that made me slightly worried.

"It would be no issue to take you back on my end," I chimed in.

"Raven will be safer here, and I don't want to put anyone on campus at risk if the kidnapper comes back and tries to finish what he started. We wouldn't want any of her roommates getting hurt because we acted too hastily. We've both been excused from campus for the time being, so I think it's wise if we stay here."

Raven turned her head and looked at Nash, and the two stared at one another.

When Bianca and I finished eating, I said, "We should head back. Some of us are playing football tomorrow and should rest up."

Nash shook his head and said, "Fine. Don't worry about the dishes, I'll grab them after I walk you two to the door."

Everyone but Raven stood up and started moving toward the door. It took a few seconds, but then she stood up too.

Bianca turned to Raven and said, "If you need anything, either one of you can text me, and I'll try my best to help. I have no issue driving out here to do it."

I coughed before I said, "Same here, but I'd prefer if it was without you though."

"Enough," Nash said, ending my argument with Bianca before it could really begin. "I'm sure we'll be fine, but we'll keep you updated."

18

BIANCA

I tugged on the hem of my burgundy dress as I scanned the room around me. Eta Sigma Nu's house was abuzz with activity as we tried to be gracious hosts for the women we were meeting today. I was trying to treat today like one of the events I attended with my parents and put my best foot forward. White string lights twinkled in several of the rooms, casting a warm glow and creating a welcoming atmosphere. The sweet aroma of the desserts we'd had catered filled the air, along with the sounds of people laughing and talking.

Jitters always accompanied the tirelessness that came with putting an event like this together. These types of events were an interview of sorts. Our guests were interested in learning more about sorority life and whether this was something they would be interested in, while we were interviewing them to see if they would be a good fit for our organization.

Being on the other side of the interviewing process now should have meant I wasn't as nervous, but something within me wouldn't let me relax. It was obvious that my nerves hated me.

"Hey, Bianca," a cheerful voice called out from behind me. I turned to find Emma, one of my sorority sisters, walking toward me with a smile that could light up a room. "Everything looks amazing! You've outdone yourself this time."

It wasn't a hardship for a smile to appear on my face about that. I'd volunteered to be the point person for this event because our sorority sister who had originally been in charge had a family emergency and needed to go back home. "Thanks, Emma. I hope everything goes smoothly tonight."

Emma placed a hand on my bare shoulder. "Everything is going to be fine. You've worked so hard, and it shows. Everyone is really excited to be here. Now, go and enjoy yourself!"

With a deep breath and Emma's words in the back of my mind, I did my best to keep my nerves at bay and tried to enjoy the festive atmosphere I'd worked hard to create. I took inspiration from my parents as I mingled with my sisters and guests, making sure to treat everyone that I came into contact with as if they were the only person here. I asked about what people were studying and what hobbies they had and repeated what they said further into the conversation to show I was interested in what they were saying. But even with the information I was gathering about the women here, I was still distracted.

Beneath the polite mask that was in place, my thoughts were anything but pleasant. Easton's piercing green eyes and teasing smirk kept flashing in my mind as I thought about how I was supposed to give him an answer today.

By the end of the event, I had identified five women who I

thought would be a great fit for Eta Sigma Nu. It was a great feeling to connect with potential and new members because, in a way, we were cementing Eta Sigma Nu's legacy and future on campus.

Temporarily, I could ignore the other problems in my life and think about the good I was doing here. But I also couldn't wait for this to be over because I wanted some time to myself.

As I was walking back into the kitchen, Emma walked in behind me and said, "I just got a text about a party that is going on tonight. We were going to wear some wigs as a way to mix things up a bit. Would you like to come with?"

I was intrigued, and it would be a way to celebrate what looked to be a huge win with this event. "I'm down." It didn't take much to convince me.

"Excellent. We have a few hours, so we can meet at my place and then head on over?"

I thought about where she lived on campus and how long it would take for me to get there from my apartment. It was a short enough distance to give me an opportunity to help with cleanup and relax before I needed to be ready to go. "Text me the details and I'll be there."

Once the event came to an end and our guests had left, I helped clean up and get everything back to normal. I said my goodbyes and thanked everyone for their help before heading home.

When I arrived at my apartment, I relaxed for a bit before I went to my closet in search of a fun outfit for the evening. While I was searching, I paused for a second because I'd finally figured out what my answer for Easton would be. Since this wasn't the time or place to think about it, I went back to looking for something to wear tonight. After much thought, I settled on a cute, sparkly, purple top and a short black leather skirt with a pair of black booties that were comfortable enough to walk around in.

Time was moving swiftly, so I took a deep breath and quickly got started with my makeup. I opted for a natural look but added a few subtle touches of bronzer to enhance my cheekbones and highlight my bare shoulders. Since the plan was for us to wear wigs, I tossed my hair up into a ponytail and figured I had plenty of time to take it down and put my hair under the wig when I got to Emma's.

Not long after, I met up with Emma and some of our sorority sisters and together, we went to the house party on campus. We arrived at the party wearing wigs that were a variety of colors. I'd picked a dark purple wig that matched my shirt, and I was happy that the wigs were a hit. Everyone that we came into contact with loved them. The party had cool vibes, and everyone seemed pretty chill, and I was happy I decided to come out and hang.

We chatted with so many different people, some that we knew and others we had never met before. The drinks were flowing, and everyone was so excited to be out and having fun.

We danced and took pictures together while we were there, and I was sure that some of them would end up on social media. I made sure that my account was private and to keep any signs of alcohol out of the pictures I was in to avoid any controversy.

The longer we stayed at this party, the more alive I felt. It was almost as if I was a new person due to feeling somewhat incognito with the wig on. As I put my beer bottle up to my lips, I realized this was the most fun I'd had out in a long time.

When the current song faded, I turned to Emma and said, "I'm going to take a quick breather, and I'll be back."

Emma gave me a short nod and I walked away, choosing to stand closer to a wall, out of the way, to catch my breath. I looked on and watched my sorority sisters having the time of their lives and it just felt good to enjoy myself too.

That was until I felt a hand cover my mouth and I was pulled in the opposite direction. I tried to scream and fight, but my attempts were futile. How had no one seen what happened? Yes, it was dark, but I hadn't realized how much so. I was pulled into a dark room, and once the door was shut behind me, the person pushed me up against the wall.

Thankfully, there was some light in the room, and it was easy to recognize who'd brought me in here: Easton.

"I want my answer, Bianca."

Why wasn't I surprised that he'd easily recognized me? "And you think dragging me into a room like an asshole is going to guarantee that you get one? Fuck you."

"Well, if you insist."

For a second we stood there, and he was standing close enough to me that we could stare into each other's eyes despite the darkness in the room. We didn't say a word. His presence was overwhelming and all-consuming. And that was before he made his move.

Easton snatched the beer out of my hand and yanked me from the wall. He pushed me back until I fell onto a bed. I gasped in response and tried to get up, but Easton yanked my legs open and pushed my skirt up.

My mouth dropped open in shock. "What the fuck—"

"If you're not going to give me an answer, I'll take it from you my way."

I jumped when I felt the glass bottle that had been in my hand only seconds before was being dragged up and down my slit. The motion, plus the change in temperature between my hot skin and the coolness of the beer bottle, was erotic.

"What's your answer, princess?"

I'd already come up with what my answer would be to his question before I stepped foot into this party. But the urge to challenge him was too strong to simply give him what he desired.

"I have no idea what you're talking about. Move so I can get up."

I could see Easton's smirk from his position between my legs. Without saying another word, I watched as he lifted the beer to his lips and took a long drink from it before he placed the bottle on the floor somewhere. The expression he wore was straight toxic and I found myself craving more of whatever he was willing to give.

What the hell was wrong with me?

Here I was, lying on a stranger's bed with my legs spread, and my brother's best friend watching my every move. He reached over and pulled down my panties, and I couldn't help but watch as he stuffed them into his pocket.

I moved to close my legs as awkwardness took over, and Easton placed his hands on my inner thighs, forcing my legs apart.

"I want to see you. All of you."

I shivered at his words and the way he stared at me. It was as if I was the only person in the world who could give him the thing he wanted most. And that was before he showed me how much he wanted me.

His mouth made a beeline for my pussy as if he needed it to ensure his survival. I sighed as he took his time playing with my clit, and when I began to squirm, he started to explore me with his tongue.

He was giving me no mercy.

Easton moved his hands from my thighs to put them in a position that wouldn't allow me to close my legs or escape from whatever he wanted to do to me. He held my hips down as he fucked me with his tongue.

The urge to scream was in the back of my throat but I was vaguely aware of where we were and who might be able to hear. Part of me didn't care, but the part that was still being held in a chokehold by my upbringing was there in my ear, telling me to stop this and warning me about what could happen if we were found.

Then something snapped within me, and I truly did not give a fuck who heard me. I could blame it on the wig, which had somehow managed to stay on my head throughout all of this, but who knows if that was the case.

My whole body was on fire as he continued to drive me wild. The pressure that was building within me couldn't continue for much longer. Everything was becoming too overwhelming, and Easton didn't miss a beat.

I clenched the bed's comforter as Easton continued his motions. My body's reactions became instinctual in nature as I felt myself reach the brink of ecstasy before Easton shoved me over the edge without bothering to slow down or stop. I groaned as my body trembled from what he'd done to me.

But even though I'd slammed through my orgasm, that didn't stop Easton from licking up every last drop.

My heart leapt into my mouth when the door burst open, and Easton stopped. My hands immediately went to my face to cover it, while Easton's hands on my body prevented me from closing my legs. I didn't know how much of me they could see with Easton's head in the way, and I was too afraid to find out.

Through my fingers, I watched as Easton turned to the guys who just burst into the room, staring open mouthed at the situation they were witnessing.

"We were looking for you, man," one of the men said.

It occurred to me that they were probably on the football team. I knew the chances of them recognizing me in the dark with this wig on were small, but damn if I didn't jump in my skin.

"Obviously, I'm fine. Can't you see I'm busy?"

The guys at the door stared for a second longer and I wondered if they were going to ask who I was before one of them elbowed the other and they left, closing the door behind them.

Then it was just Easton and me in the room alone once more. He gave my pussy one more lick before he pulled away and closed my legs together.

"Now, where were we? Oh, I was asking you what your answer to my offer was."

I took a deep breath and gave him the answer he'd been waiting for. "Yes."

19

BIANCA

I was shaking my body to the latest pop song while I washed some dishes in my apartment. I'd already finished classes for the day, and after that, I had a chapter meeting that was unusually short. I was determined to do what I could to somewhat have my shit together.

Plus, for whatever reason, cleaning up made me feel better about how my life was currently going, so here I was.

I'd relived the moment with Easton at the party more times than I could count. He hadn't said a word to me since that night, and I couldn't help but feel somewhat annoyed about the whole thing. I guess I'd expected him to be all in, calling me and texting me immediately, but when he didn't, I couldn't help but wonder what had gone wrong. I had no intention of reaching out to him, but him keeping his distance just felt strange. Normally, I would be grateful to not have to deal with him, but since this deal had been struck, now I was wondering if he had some sort of trick up his sleeve to make me lose my shit. Or if this was another little game that he was starting to play, and I was going to be in for it.

When my phone buzzed on the counter brought me out of my thoughts, I looked over at my screen, and when I saw that Iris's name had popped up on it, I immediately answered. "Hello."

"Bianca?"

"What's wrong?" I asked as I put away a glass that I'd just washed.

"I—I have something I need to tell you."

I narrowed my gaze. Something sounded wrong, and I didn't like what I was hearing. "Do you want me to come over? This sounds like something that needs to be said in person versus over the phone."

"No, I'd rather come to you, if you aren't busy."

That wouldn't be a bad idea, I thought before another thought popped into my brain. "I don't have anything going on. Why don't you pack a bag, and you can stay with me overnight? We can order takeout and some junk food."

It was almost the weekend and would give us an opportunity to hang out. It was a great idea.

"Okay. When do you want me to come over?" Iris's voice shook slightly.

All of this was only increasing my concern about what could have happened to her. "Whenever is good."

"How about in forty-five minutes?"

That worked for me. "I'll see you then."

When Iris hung up the phone, I went back to washing my dishes. I had a few minutes to do a couple of things to make my home homier for Iris, and thankfully, I didn't think any of the tasks would take long.

Once I was done with the dishes, I tidied up the living room, grabbed two of the blankets I kept in the closet, and tossed them on the couch in case she wanted to watch movies or something. We had some snacks that we could eat, and plenty to drink. If there was anything we didn't have, I had no problem having it delivered.

I hopped into the shower to do a quick refresh ahead of Iris's arrival, and by the time I was dressed in my usual attire and had thrown my hair up into a messy bun, I got a text message from her saying that she'd just arrived and to meet her at the front desk.

I grabbed the keys to my apartment and left, eager to get downstairs and see Iris. When I spotted her, I stared her down as she walked through the glass door that led to my apartment's lobby. I swallowed hard as I took in the look on her face. It gave away just how serious whatever it was that happened to her.

I didn't say a word as I opened my arms to let Iris step into them.

"Come on. Let's get you upstairs," I said.

All she did was nod, but she looked as if she might cry at any moment.

I gave a small wave to the person working at the front desk as she gave a small nod, and together, we took the elevator up to my apartment.

I threw my keys down on the counter and grabbed Iris's duffel bag to give her a hand. She sunk down into the cushions and I pulled a soft quilt over her body. She looked downright exhausted, and I wished I could do more.

I left Iris on the couch and walked toward the kitchen. "Is there anything I can get you?"

"Some water would be nice."

"Coming up."

I moved around the kitchen when an idea popped in my head. Water wasn't going to do the trick for this. I grabbed four glasses and filled them with ice. While I was moving around the kitchen, I debated telling her about Easton, but didn't think now was the right time. I then grabbed a bottle of white wine out of my wine fridge and poured it over the ice. Was ice and wine controversial? Maybe, but at least we would have a cold, refreshing drink. I poured water into the other two and then grabbed the glasses of wine. As I walked back to the living room with the two wine glasses, Iris was putting the remote back down on the coffee table.

"This isn't water, Bianca," she said as I set a glass down in front of her.

"I know it's not. I'll be grabbing that next, but it sounded like this story required something a little stronger." I turned on my heel and strolled back to the kitchen to retrieve the other two glasses, setting them next to the glasses of wine.

I sat down next to Iris and grabbed my glass of wine. After I took a sip, I looked at her and said, "Now tell me what's going on. You have me worried."

Iris drank a big gulp of her wine and almost choked. I moved to pat her on the back, but she recovered before I could do anything. She put the glass down on the coffee table once again.

"Are you ready to talk now?" I asked before I took another sip.

She nodded and ran both of her hands across her face. "Someone is stalking me."

Iris refused to look me in the eye for some reason. I

wondered if she was embarrassed by admitting this to me. I could see her vulnerability and my heart broke for her.

I cleared my throat and said, "Stalking, as in, someone is following you? Tracking your movements?"

"Yeah. He is also the one who sent me the laptop."

She glanced at me as my eyes widened. It was a miracle my mouth hadn't dropped open yet.

I shook my head in disbelief. "I have so many questions, but I don't understand why anyone would do that. You keep to yourself and do your best not to attract attention. Have you gone to campus security about it?"

"I wish I knew why. It started at the beginning of the year, and he's broken into my room twice now, and yes, I've gone to campus security."

I did a double take. I put my wine on the coffee table next to Iris's. I reached over and grabbed Iris by her forearms and slightly shook her. "What's his name? Screw campus security, we need to go to the police."

"No. He hasn't mentioned his name. I'm afraid to go to the cops because he threatened to harm Gran."

I watched as she teared up. Threatening her grandma's well-being would do that to her. One tear escaped and fell from the corner of her eye.

Iris gathered herself and continued. "He knows where she lives, and I know that because he was able to recite her address to me and, supposedly, he took a picture of her home. Hell, I don't know if I'm doing the wrong thing here by telling you right now. I can't afford to have anything happen to Gran."

I removed my hands from her forearms and pulled her toward me, hugging her as tightly as I could. I held her like that for what felt like forever, and I hoped it was providing even a small sense of comfort during this troubling time for her.

Iris sniffled and said, "I don't know what he wants, and I don't know why he continues harassing me. I have nothing to give."

"That's not true. You have plenty to give, and to the people that know you, you mean the world to them. Don't let him force you to question your worth."

She pulled back and looked at me but didn't say a word. That might have been the most profound thing I'd ever said to her in the years we'd known each other.

I stood up and walked into the kitchen again. Iris was in the middle of finishing her wine when I walked back over to the couch with a paper towel in hand to help her wipe her face.

"I still think going to the police is the best bet here. We don't know how dangerous this guy is."

"I can't."

"I had a feeling you'd say that. Going back to campus security is an option. Maybe they can do more patrols near your dorm room and see if they can spot him at least. Have you seen him clearly and can describe him?"

"I've already talked to campus security, and they are supposedly working with the police to find him. And yes, I know what he looks like."

"At least we have that to go on, and the police do know," my voice trailed off as I swiped a piece of hair behind my ear after it fell out of my messy bun. "I'll talk to my parents about it. Maybe they know someone who knows what you could possibly do in this situation."

"If you're okay with doing that."

I wiped my hands on my sweatpants. "I don't like going to them for things if I can avoid it, but you clearly need help, and I want to do all that I can."

"Okay. Is it alright if I go..." she gestured to the bathroom instead of trying to finish her sentence.

"Of course."

I watched as she walked away before I grabbed my wine, and then I folded my legs under my body. I didn't know what I could do about this outside of going to my parents for help. If the stalker was a member of this community, then the chances were high that my mother or father knew them. But would they be willing to help, given them not caring for my relationship with Iris?

Not to mention we didn't know her stalker's name.

Times like this made me wish that she either attended Brentson, or that I'd gone to Westwick. Being on the same campus would be beneficial when it came to this, not to mention we would get to see each other more.

I took another sip of my wine and sighed. The seriousness of this weighed on me and I couldn't imagine how Iris was feeling about all of it. I told myself I would do whatever it took to make sure that she and her grandma didn't get hurt, but we were battling the unknown, with no end in sight.

20

BIANCA

When I walked into my psychology class, something felt very different. I couldn't pinpoint what made me feel this way, but I could feel it, nonetheless.

"Good morning, Bianca," Dr. Chen greeted me as I walked past.

Dr. Chen's energy was odd as she stood up at the front of the classroom, and I wondered what type of surprise she was going to drop on us today.

"Good morning, Dr. Chen," I replied cautiously, wondering what could be going on. Was it something about today's lesson? Had I missed something important?

As I settled into my seat, I glanced around the room. Everything seemed normal as my classmates prepared for today's lesson. As my eyes glanced at the door, Easton walked in. Although I'd seen him since that party, my mind immediately drifted back to that night when he made me absolutely lose control.

Shit. I don't need to be thinking about him in that way right now.

"Alright, everyone, let's get started," Dr. Chen called out, stopping my thoughts in their tracks.

"Today, we'll be tackling a new project," she continued. "And I think putting you into groups of two is the best way to handle this task."

My stomach did a somersault when she said partners. I hated working in groups. Working with someone else always caused my anxiety to go through the roof. Having to depend on other people made me feel as if I was getting hives.

Please don't pair me with Easton. I glanced at the man who occupied my thoughts, but I didn't say a word out loud. The last thing I needed was to be forced to spend more time with him.

"Once I tell you who your partner is, take a moment to discuss your ideas with each other," Dr. Chen said. She started walking around the class, telling people who they would be partnered with and handing out case studies. My nerves were completely shot as I watched her tell everyone who they would be working with.

"Alright, let's see," as she read from the piece of paper in her hand. "Bianca, you'll be working with... Easton."

I would have sworn my heart stopped beating if I hadn't still been alive. The universe just told me to go back to bed and try again tomorrow.

"You've got to be shitting me," I muttered under my breath as Easton turned around to face me. The intensity in his eyes shook me to my core.

"Hey, Bianca," he said as a wicked grin played at the

corners of his mouth. "I'm looking forward to working with you."

I tried to swallow the lump in my throat, wondering if he'd somehow orchestrated this. I wouldn't be surprised if he had.

Come on, Bianca. He can't control Dr. Chen's decisions.

"Sure," I said, my voice barely audible. "Let's get this over with."

Dr. Chen cleared her throat and said, "Your assignment will be to analyze a case study of an individual suffering from a psychological disorder. You'll need to explore the root causes, symptoms, and treatments for the disorder, as well as the ethical considerations involved in its study and treatment."

"As far as a due date," Dr. Chen continued, "this project must be completed by the end of the semester. I expect a polished final product because it is worth twenty percent of your final grade."

Fuck. I can't even half ass it because it's such a big percentage of my grade.

"Okay, everyone has a partner now. We can get started," Dr. Chen announced before she gave us more instructions about how we were supposed to carry out this project.

Once Dr. Chen wrapped up her comments, Easton and I began to discuss the project. Even with us remaining professional, I could still feel the tension that continued to brew between us. This whole thing was going to be a hot mess.

"So, how do you want to split up the work?" I asked.

"Let's see," he paused for a moment, I assumed to think of a response. "How about you handle the research and I'll take care of the... presentation?"

"By *presentation*, do you mean writing too?" I tried to make it clear that he wasn't going to throw the bulk of the work at me and get off easy.

"Of course," he said as I saw some sincerity in his eyes. "I'll put in just as much work as you do."

"Good, and we'll need to communicate to make sure we're on the same page, and to get status updates about how we are doing."

"Deal," he said as he put his hand out for me to shake. Although I thought this was ridiculous, I also stuck my hand out, and as soon as our hands touched, a jolt passed through my body. I wanted to pull mine back but Easton's grasp on my hand kept me in place.

"Sounds perfect to me," he replied, his voice low to the point I was questioning whether I'd heard him correctly. "I look forward to talking to you more, Bianca."

As the clock ticked away, Dr. Chen made her way around the room, providing feedback to each group. I tried to focus on what she was saying, but my mind was all too happy to think about Easton and the precarious positions we'd been put in.

I pulled out my laptop and began typing what we talked about into a shared Google Doc. Given how distracted I was, it was best to put everything down there so it would be easy to recall what was discussed.

"Okay," Dr. Chen said, as she walked past us, nodding in approval at our progress.

"Thanks for pairing us up, Dr. Chen," Easton replied, smirking at me. "Bianca and I are great at finding common ground and working together, aren't we?"

I clenched my jaw as I tried to ignore his innuendos. "What he means is, we can't wait to start this."

"Great, I'm glad to hear that," Dr. Chen affirmed, moving on to the next pair.

As she walked away, I turned to glare at Easton. He was getting on my damn nerves.

"We're going to have to exchange phone numbers," Easton said as if it weren't a big deal.

I debated whether it was something I should do. It made sense for us to exchange contact information for this project, but I was giving him another way to access me. Phone numbers would be easier than email and it wasn't like he couldn't get my number from Nash. However, my brother would ask more questions before giving it up.

I sighed as I pulled out my phone and handed it to him. He quickly typed in his number and then called himself, so he had my number as well.

"Alright, how about we meet up at Beyond The Page tomorrow after class to work on our research," Easton suggested. It was the first thing he'd said since this project was announced that made sense.

"Sure," I replied as I pulled out my phone to add it to my calendar. "Would 6:30 p.m. work?"

"That should be fine. I can't do the following day because of..." Easton's voice trailed off.

"Because of what?" My curiosity got the better of me even though I had no business asking about his schedule.

"I've just got something to do that has come up."

The secrecy about what he was doing shouldn't have made me more curious, but here I was, wondering what he was doing that had him preoccupied this week. His dark hair fell across his forehead before he pushed it away from his face, adding to the mysterious aura that surrounded him and now this thing he didn't want to tell me about. Not that he had to tell me anything, of course. Or so I tried to tell myself.

"I hope everything is okay." I looked at him as I wondered if he would take the hint and give me more to go on.

I vaguely heard Dr. Chen dismiss us, and my classmates gathering their things to leave the classroom.

"It is, you don't need to worry, even though it's cute that you are," he said. Before I could respond, he added, "See you tomorrow, Bianca."

"See you then," I said as I watched him gather his things and leave the classroom. As soon as he was out of sight, I let out a deep breath before I began to pack my own things.

My brain couldn't figure out what to focus on because it seemed as if nothing made sense. He still hadn't brought up the deal we struck, and now we were forced to work together on a class project. Fear tore through me because I didn't know what to expect when it came to any of this. What should I do?

Going with the flow when it came to this was probably the best bet, but throughout all of it, I felt as if I was five steps behind everyone else.

Which made me want to sink into a bottle of wine.

As I grabbed my bookbag and put the strap over my shoulder, I was convinced that there was no way Easton and I would be able to work together. But I had to try to remain on my best behavior because our grades depended on it.

However, there was no way that I couldn't bring up the offer. It was bothering me that he hadn't acted on it, and I needed to know more in order to better prepare myself.

As I fought with myself about how I felt about all of this, I gave Dr. Chen a small wave and left the class, wondering how much she'd screwed me by partnering me up with Easton for this project.

21

EASTON

Beyond The Page buzzed with activity, and the aroma of fresh coffee and pastries wafted through the air. I tapped my pen on the surface of the corner table I'd been sitting at for the last twenty minutes and checked my phone for the tenth time.

Where was she? Bianca hadn't mentioned that she would be late.

Before I could remove my hand, my phone vibrated in my palm, and I noticed who was calling me.

"What's up, Nash?"

"Are you still able to come tomorrow?"

I nodded to myself before I responded, "Yeah, I'll be there."

"See you then," he hung up before I could say anything else.

Nash and I had been on a roller coaster of an adventure since Raven, his ex-girlfriend, now current girlfriend or whatever they'd decided on at this point, came back to Brenston.

The deeper things got, the more I'd gotten glimpses of the

Chevaliers, the secret society that Nash was involved in, and the one that I was potentially going to go through recruitment/initiation for.

That's what tomorrow would hopefully be the start of.

My thoughts were snatched from me when my gaze flickered to the entrance as Bianca walked in. She scanned the room and her eyes met mine, a frown present on her beautiful face. She looked to be okay, which caused relief to flow through my body.

It was then I realized I'd been worried about her.

Bianca made her way over to my table and I couldn't help but be mesmerized by the sway of her hips. The urge to grab her by those very hips and pull her down on my cock was high.

Fuck. I need to control myself.

With a loud sigh, I shoved aside my inappropriate thoughts. We were here to work on our group project, not to think about the times I made her come hard.

"You're late," I said as Bianca slid into the seat across from me. Was I being a bit harsh? Sure, but I didn't care.

"Hello to you too, Easton." Her tone dripped with sarcasm.

Deep down, I knew it was in response to how I spoke to her first, but that knowledge did little to quell my irritation.

"Can we please just get to work?"

Bianca's eyes flashed. "That's the same plan I had. I don't know what went up your ass and died but—"

"I got here at 6:30 p.m. ready to work, and you weren't here. You're wasting my time," I leaned forward, lowering my voice. "Now, are you going to help with this project or not?"

She mirrored my posture, her face inches from mine. I

couldn't resist staring at her lips before she spoke. "I'll help you with this, *if* you pull that stick out of your ass."

I fought the urge to kiss that smug look right off her face. That wouldn't be appropriate. Then again, tongue-fucking her in someone else's bed wasn't appropriate either, and I was very proud of that moment.

It might have been the hottest thing I'd ever seen.

I swallowed hard, heat pooling in my gut at our proximity. Damn it, I needed to focus.

"This tension between us," I said softly, "it's not just about this project, and you know it. The deal we struck is causing even more problems than we already have."

Bianca's eyes widened, but she didn't pull away. "I've been waiting for you to bring it up."

"The deal?"

All Bianca did was nod her head.

"Yes, the deal. By the look on your face, you seem surprised." I wanted to reach out and touch her, but we were in public and who knew who was watching. "Let's talk about the deal briefly, and then we have to get to work."

"Sure, but I'm only agreeing with you because I want to get this over and done with so we can both move on. We also never spoke about a timeframe for when all this would end."

She was right and I needed to come up with an answer fast. "Until the end of the semester. Right around the time this project is due because it will also give us a cover for why we are spending time together. No one will be the wiser."

"Did you really just pull that out of your ass?"

I nodded, slightly happy with myself. "Are you impressed?"

"I am and if this keeps those..." Bianca looked around

before she continued, "photos from getting out, then I will do it."

Our eyes connected and I wished I could make all this go away. Deciding to blackmail Bianca wasn't the first option I would choose to do in order to get her to spend time with me, but I was determined to win no matter what. "Let's get to work."

Bianca nodded, agreeing with me, and we set about the task of reading over the case study and taking notes. We kept it professional, although our stares met for longer than required, and I could feel the energy between the two of us, showing just how explosive things would be when we collided again.

After about an hour, I looked up from my laptop. "Do you want anything to drink? I'm going to grab something."

Bianca glared at me for a moment before her gaze softened at my unexpected question, and she smiled. "Sure, that would be nice. Can I get a coffee?"

"Decaf? Cream? Two sugars?"

She stared at me for a moment and said, "Yes to all those things. How do you know how I take my coffee?"

I shrugged. "It was just a guess." It wasn't really, I just remembered how she'd ordered it before.

I moved so that I could get up and walked over to the coffee shop portion of Beyond The Page and stood at the counter, but no one was there. After waiting there for a few moments, I walked away and came across a woman restocking books in one of the aisles. She looked up before I could walk away.

"Is there anything I can help you with?"

I glanced down at her name tag and saw that her name

was Harlow. "I'm just looking for whoever is running the coffee station."

Harlow checked her watch before she said, "Courtnay should be back... right now."

Just as the words left her lips, I watched as someone circled the counter before stopping behind it.

"Thanks."

Harlow gave me a smile and then said, "It was no trouble at all."

I turned and walked back to the barista and ordered two decaf coffees and some cake pops as a small snack for both Bianca and me. Once everything was ready, I paid and walked back to where I left Bianca and our things. Her eyes lit up when she saw me.

"Coffee and cake pops... is this a date?"

Her hands flew up to her face as if she was shocked that the words came out of her mouth. Her eyes were as wide as saucers, and I was sure that behind her hands she was blushing.

I shook my head. "I don't date."

My words seemed to pull Bianca out of her stupor. "What do you mean, you don't date?"

I shrugged as I gestured for her to pick which cake pop she wanted. When she did, I took the other and sat down. "I don't date. There's nothing more to it."

"Have you been celibate then?"

I scoffed. "Absolutely not. I just don't date anyone."

It was kind of funny watching it all click for Bianca because the range of expressions that crossed her face was comical. While I waited for her to reply, she did the opposite, instead choosing to stuff the cake pop into her mouth.

It took her a moment to chew, swallow, and wash the food down with some of the coffee. Then Bianca asked, "So why don't you date?"

I shrugged in response. "I guess I just don't believe in the whole idea. The time that you need to put into making relationships work could be better used elsewhere. I prefer to keep things casual and take things as they come. No strings attached, if you will."

"But aren't your parents happily married?"

"They are as far as I know."

"Then did a relationship that you had color your outlook on this?"

"Nope. I've never been in a relationship."

That news seemed to surprise her, but she didn't say anything, instead choosing to take another drink of her hot coffee.

Bianca coughed and then spoke. "I guess that makes sense. I mean, I get where you're coming from, but there are those relationships that last for decades because both parties worked hard at making it happen, and then there's also the reward at the end when two people finally find their happy ending."

I shrugged and nodded my head in understanding. I could see where she was coming from too, but I still wasn't convinced that dating was something I wanted to do.

Before I could respond, Bianca changed the subject and asked about our progress on the psychology project. We spent the next few minutes going over what we'd done and what we still needed to do.

By the time we were finished talking about the project, our cake pops were long gone and most of our coffee was as well. Bianca moved to gather her things, and I followed by packing my stuff up.

After we'd cleaned up, I walked her to her car. She turned to face me before she got into her vehicle.

"Bianca, for the first part of our deal, I want you to wear my jersey to the football game on Saturday. We can see each other after the game."

Her eyes widened as she leaned forward slightly. "B-but I thought—"

"You thought the deal only had to do with sex?"

She nodded once before she looked down at the ground for a moment. Her eyes shot back up to me, and she said, "I can't wear your jersey on Saturday. I don't have one and it would make people suspicious."

"You can say you lost a bet."

Her gaze narrowed on me. "I'll think about it."

I didn't say that there would be consequences for not obeying what I wanted, but she'd find out soon enough.

Bianca got into her car. Before she closed the door behind her, I said, "I'll see you on Saturday."

"Maybe."

She closed the door, and I moved back so that she could drive off.

As I watched her slowly drive away, I told myself I needed to shove thoughts of her out of my mind and focus on what needed to happen tomorrow.

22

BIANCA

Football.

It always made me nervous.

Having been to more of Nash's football games than I could count, I still couldn't stop the nerves I got every time he took the field. But at least I wasn't alone.

"Hey, Raven. Can I ask you something?"

Raven turned to look at me and gave me a wide smile. She and I decided that we would attend today's game together, and I invited Iris along with us. It would give her an opportunity to get off Westwick's main campus for a bit, which she needed with her stalker still roaming around.

"Sure. What's up?"

"Did you get the invite to the luncheon?"

"What luncheon?"

"The one that my sorority is hosting. I asked them to invite you, and I noticed you weren't there, so I didn't know if you'd gotten left off the guest list or what," I said.

"I did get the invite, but with everything going on..."

She made an excellent point. "It's fine, and I completely

understand. But I wanted you to know that we did extend an invitation to you in case you wanted to come and see what we are all about. Just let me know. It would be a bit more informal than if it were our regular recruitment, but..."

She nodded and smiled. "I'll definitely let you know, Bianca. Thank you."

We both turned back to the game, and we watched as Nash threw a pass to Easton, and Easton took off down the field.

I glanced down at the jersey I had on before I looked back at the game and said, "Part of me wants to root for him because I'll be rooting for the Bears, but it's also fucking *him*."

I could see Raven turned her head slightly to look at me. "You hate him that much, huh?"

"You don't even know."

"Does your brother know how much you dislike him?"

I shrugged. "I don't think so. He probably thinks it's more along the lines of him treating me like a kid sister, but..." There was so much Nash didn't know.

Raven waited a beat before she said, "Do you want to talk about it?"

"Nope," I said as I shook my head. "That's a story for another day, and we should be focusing on the game."

I drew my attention to the field and a few minutes later, I said, "You know what?"

"What?"

"Being in the presence of anything related to Westwick University freaks me out."

"Why is that?"

I shrugged. "I think it's the vibe that the school gives off that has rubbed off on me the wrong way. I visited Iris there once and it almost felt like a dark cloud was over the school. I feel bad for Iris because she has to go there. She's the one who is supposed to be meeting us here."

"She can't transfer to Brentson?" Raven asked.

I shook her head. "Nope. It's family tradition for her to go to Westwick, so she's doing it."

I didn't elaborate any more, because I didn't want to tell more of Iris's story than I should. It wasn't my place to tell anyway. A cold breeze blew, and I shivered under the jersey I was wearing and the coat I threw over it.

I was freezing my butt off in this stupid jersey and I was regretting the choices I'd made.

"Bianca?"

I jumped and turned to face the person that called my name. I couldn't fight the grin that took over my face.

"Iris, hey!" I quickly pulled her into my arms before she had a chance to react. When we broke apart, I gestured to the woman standing beside me. "Iris, this is Raven. She's my brother's girlfriend. Raven, this is my friend, Iris."

"It's nice to meet you," Iris said as they shook hands.

"Likewise," Raven replied. "I'll move down and you can sit on the other side of Bianca."

I was happy that Raven and Iris had the opportunity to meet. I moved so that Iris could get comfortable and turned my attention back to the game momentarily.

When my phone rang, I pulled it out and saw that it was a text message. I reread the message repeatedly, but I refused to show any emotion on my face. I didn't know if the person who sent me the text message was watching me or not.

Instead, I shrugged my shoulders and showed the message to Iris before I handed my phone to Raven so that she too could read the message. I was freaked out, but I refused to show it.

> Unknown Number: Be careful what you wish for, B.

Maybe it wouldn't hurt to tell Nash about this, because telling the police was the last thing I was planning to do. It would lead to my parents getting involved and that was not something I wanted to deal with. But with Iris being stalked, I needed to be careful. Could it be the same person?

Westwick and Brentson were close, so it wouldn't be outside the realm of possibility for whoever it was to be stalking us both. But given what Iris said, whoever was texting me hadn't taken it to the extremes that her stalker had. So, at least there was that.

What also confused me was what the hell had I wished for?

I'd wished not to have to deal with my father's career or Easton after the way he treated me years ago. But not many people knew about my feelings toward either of those things. So, I was lost, and none of this made any sense.

Then again, what did make sense in my life nowadays?

I shrugged off the unknown number's message and refocused my attention on the football game. Raven, Iris, and I talked quietly as we watched the game, but the excitement was building. The score was close. The crowd roared with excitement as each play brought us one step closer to the conclusion of the game.

We were up by two points in the fourth quarter when Raven nudged my shoulder, and I was convinced it was because she was nervous. Nash was doing well, making accurate passes, and the rest of the team was doing their part against their division rivals. As if on cue, Westwick's quarterback threw an interception that turned the tide of the game. The stadium cheered as our team scored two more touchdowns to clinch their victory.

"Thank goodness," I said as I listened to the cheers around me erupt when the clock hit zero. It took some time for the stadium to clear out and for us to make it to where the Bears were.

It took even longer for the football players to exit, but as soon as I saw Nash, I knew what was going to happen. When Raven and Nash's eyes met, it was game over. She turned to smile at me and Iris briefly. We nodded our heads as I saw Nash jogging toward her, and soon he pulled her into his arms and gave her a huge kiss. I couldn't help but be happy for them, especially after everything they'd been through. It was wonderful to see my brother happy again.

"I'm going to head out, okay?"

I turned to look at Iris after she spoke. "Are you sure? I can take you back to Westwick?"

I was referring to the fact that there was a stalker on the loose and who seemed to be taking things up a notch every time she told me a new story. It was also the reason why I didn't mention anything about Easton because she had enough on her plate.

"I'm okay. I drove here from my dorm and there are still plenty of people and security around, so I feel safe."

"If you're sure."

"I'm sure."

"Well, text me when you get back to your dorm."

I gave her a big hug and waved to her as she walked away.

My brother and Raven were still quietly talking with one another, and it was then I realized Easton hadn't shown his face yet. What the hell was taking him so long?

"Bianca," I heard, and I turned to find my brother and Raven now watching me. I turned my body so I could give him a high-five.

"Excellent game today."

"Thanks. There were some things we could improve on, but overall, it was a great game."

I nodded in agreement. "It was a nail-biter a few times for sure."

I barely heard my phone over the loud noises that were carrying on around me.

> Easton: I'll be out in a few. Wait for me.

For some reason, reading those words sent my body into a panic. What was he going to have me do?

"Everything okay?"

I looked up, startled, at Raven who had a look of concern on her face. Nash was looking at me curiously as well, as if he was trying to figure out what was up.

"Yeah, everything is fine," I lied as I swallowed hard.

My mind felt as if it was in a free fall with no end in sight. How was any of this going to work with Easton, with Nash and Raven right here?

As if I'd summoned him, I saw Easton walking toward us, looking every bit the bad boy that I knew him to be. His eyes were clearly on me, focused on my torso and the jersey I was wearing. When he walked up to us, he gave Raven a small, short hug, and then turned to me with a smirk on his face. I dared him to hug me, and he wisely chose not to.

"Shit, we have reservations at a restaurant, and we're already cutting it close because of how long it took to get out here. We also have to drop Bianca off."

"I can do that," Easton volunteered.

Of course, he could.

"Not to worry. I can find my own way back."

"That's silly," Easton said. "I'll do it, and it's not a problem."

"Only if you're sure," Nash said as he looked at Easton and then me for confirmation.

"It's fine," I said, not wanting to be the cause of my brother and his girlfriend missing their date.

"Come on," Nash said, breaking the tension. "Let's get out of here and get something to eat. Thanks for taking Bianca home, man."

"It's not an issue."

Nash grabbed Raven's hand and began pulling her toward the door.

Raven shot me a look of understanding before she allowed Nash to take her away. "We'll leave you two alone," she said with a knowing smirk before turning back to face Nash. "Now come on, let's go!"

And then they were gone, leaving me alone with Easton. Our eyes met for a moment, and I felt as if my heart was about to burst out of my chest. Taking a deep breath, I forced myself to focus on his face and stay calm.

For what felt like an eternity, there was silence between us as we just stared at each other, neither one of us saying a word. It was as if there was no one else but us in the world, even though there were plenty of people around us. Easton spun in a circle and then started walking away.

I jogged a couple of steps to catch up with him and I said, "You could have given me a warning before you started walking away."

"I'm keeping you on your toes," he replied.

I rolled my eyes in response, and we stayed quiet until we exited the stadium and were at his car. Easton opened the back seat of his SUV and stuck his gym bag inside. He then walked around and opened the passenger-side door to let me in.

He eyed me suspiciously and said, "That's not the jersey I told you to wear."

I looked down at the jersey I had on, and smirked because it was my brother's number. I shifted my gaze to look back at Easton. "I'm here, aren't I? You should be happy with that."

Easton's gaze narrowed at me. "When it comes to the deal we struck, I expect you to obey what I said."

I chuckled humorlessly. "You can't be serious. I don't do the whole Neanderthal shit."

"Wouldn't it be nice to not have to worry about anything other than coming all over my fingers, my tongue, and my cock?" He paused and studied me hard as his words sunk in. "You just might like giving up control. Not having to worry about anything besides the pleasure I'm going to give you. Get into the car, princess."

I stared at him for a moment before I decided to get into the vehicle, and I prayed to myself that I was going to have the ride of my life.

23

EASTON

I gripped the steering wheel hard enough for my knuckles to turn white as I drove back to Brentson University. Beside me, Bianca gazed out the window, but I could feel every so often that her eyes would land on me, like she was watching to see what I would say or do next.

I swallowed hard as I tried to focus on the road ahead. The only thing that filled my mind was Bianca's soft skin, her breathy moans, and the taste that was uniquely her.

This deal had been something that had been at the forefront of my mind even as the rest of my life had steadily gotten more complicated. I'd intentionally waited a while to act because it would keep her on her toes, and she wouldn't know what was coming or when. I wasn't even sure if she knew what was going to happen now. However, I had no doubt in my mind she would figure out that something was up as soon as I turned off the main road to Brentson. I had something to take care of before I took her home. I tapped my finger on the steering wheel to the beat of the music, and then put on my turn signal.

It took a moment for Bianca to realize what was happening, but when she did, she asked "Where are we going? This isn't the way to campus."

"We're taking a short detour."

I turned, kept driving us further into the woods, scanning for the place I'd found before. It took a few minutes, but soon, we were driving up to a parking lot that was a place where people parked to go hiking. I drove to the far corner, nowhere near the entrance of the hiking trail, but also slightly hidden in the shadows due to the trees that were nearby. It was the perfect spot for what I had planned.

I put the car into park, killed the engine, but left the car on. I turned the heat on low and turned off the music, leaving Bianca and me in complete silence.

Would it have been easier to take her back to my place or her apartment to do this? Sure, but I couldn't wait that long. I unbuckled my seat belt but didn't say a word.

Bianca turned to me, a questioning look in her eyes. "What are we doing here?"

I reached out and grabbed her jaw sternly but without hurting her. "I couldn't wait anymore, Bianca. I need you. Now."

Her eyes widened, and I wondered if she was going to fight me. But then she visibly relaxed. Her surprised expression turned into a warm grin. "Then fuck me."

"With pleasure."

Her words were the only invitation I needed. I tipped her head up slightly before our lips crashed together. It felt as if our kiss was something I couldn't quantify with words. What I did know was that once my lips were on hers, my body felt as if it was ablaze, and the only thing that could extinguish the burning desire was her. My hands moved from her face down her body briefly, until I came into contact with the item that was restricting her movement: her seat belt.

We were forced to break apart temporarily as she took off the seat belt to gain more freedom with her movement.

Not being able to touch her for those few seconds was too long, but as she was moving, an idea popped into my head. "Take off the jersey and pants."

She looked at me curiously and said, "Wait what?"

"Take them off and then climb over here and sit on my lap."

She stared at my crotch for a moment and then looked up at me. "Are you sure?"

"I've never been more sure about anything in my life." And neither had my cock.

"But what if someone sees us?"

"Isn't that the exciting part about all of this? The potential to get caught?"

I reached into my gym bag laying on the back seat and pulled out a condom. I tossed it into one of the cup holders and looked over at her once more. She bit the corner of her lip, I assumed, debating my words. To help her make her decision faster, I said, "You have fifteen seconds to get your ass over here, and if you don't, I'm adding it to the punishment I already have for you."

"What?"

"You didn't think I would punish you for wearing your brother's jersey when I said to wear mine? Fifteen... fourteen..."

Her movements would have been comical if I hadn't been turned on. She shoved her coat and jersey off and took off her shoes in record time, but her tight jeans were giving her trouble. I couldn't say that I minded because I loved watching her tits jiggle in the tight white tank top she'd decided to wear under the jersey. I'd lost count as I watched her finally peel the clothes from her body, and I wished it had been me with my hands on her.

I pushed my seat down slightly as she was removing the offending articles of clothing. Once she was in nothing but the tank top, bra, and panties, she climbed over the center console as gracefully as she could before she sat on my lap. Before she was able to get properly situated, my fingers had woven themselves into her hair as I brought her lips down to mine once again. I couldn't stop the groan that left my lips as I got another taste of her.

The guilt about this secret fling danced in the back of my mind, but it was hard for me to give a shit. All that mattered was Bianca and the way we felt in this moment. I deepened the kiss, giving in to my desire to consume her. In this moment, she was mine, and that thought was all consuming.

Bianca moaned into my mouth as my hands slipped under her tank top. The sound was like music to my ears, a sound I never wanted to forget. As my hands moved, her tank top followed suit until I was tracing the lace on her bra, teasing her as I went. She arched into my touch and cried out.

"Easton," she said against my lips.

I waited for her to continue, but it was as if any other thoughts had died once she said my name. That was fine though because I knew what we both wanted and needed right now.

I pulled the tank top off her body as it was presented to me. I allowed my hands to roam all over her skin, trying to memorize every touch and sensation. Being able to touch her and draw out every ounce of pleasure from her felt like a privilege I would never regret. My fingers reached behind her to find the clasp of her bra as I laid another kiss on her lips. The straps fell away with ease, and I laid back to get another look at her.

Even before she took her clothes off, I knew she was the most beautiful woman I'd ever seen. Hell, I knew it when I caught her eye at the party her parents hosted years ago. I couldn't help myself as I brushed my thumb over one nipple, and she trembled into my touch.

"You're so fucking beautiful," I said hoarsely. "If I don't see all of you, I don't know what I'll do."

It was cute to watch as a blush appeared on her cheeks, but there was something else I quickly noticed. Her eyes, the bright blue I'd become accustomed to, had turned darker. Arousal filled them, and I couldn't wait to explore her more.

"You have way too many clothes on, Easton," she said, smiling.

She had a good point. Bianca moved back slightly, giving me enough room to unzip the hoodie I'd thrown on after my shower, along with the Brentson Bears t-shirt I'd put on. Her eyes studied my chest just before she gave herself permission to explore. Feeling her touch across my skin was enough to make me short-circuit and all I wanted to do was—

I stopped thinking and just acted. I grabbed her ponytail and pulled, forcing her head back and chest up, making it easier to suck a nipple into my mouth. I rolled her other nipple between my fingers, enjoying the sigh that escaped from her mouth.

I leant away from and slapped her tit lightly. She gasped

in surprise, and I said, "That's for wearing Nash's jersey instead of mine."

"Don't you think it would have been suspicious for me to wear yours and not my brother's?"

I slapped her tit again and she groaned. "You could have come up with a good excuse."

I took her nipple back into my mouth and her head fell back. Doing this in the small confines of the driver's seat added another dimension to fucking that I hadn't been expecting. But maybe that also had to do with the fact that we were fucking in public.

Her moans were going to be the death of me, I was sure. The adrenaline I felt during the game earlier had transformed into another form, and the only relief I would get would be from sticking my cock into her pussy.

Speaking of, I switched breasts and allowed my fingers to make their way from her nipple, down her stomach, and further down until I reached her pussy. The look in her eyes captivated me, and it wasn't until I moved her soaked panties to the side that I bothered to look down at the sight that greeted me.

"How are you already this wet, princess?"

"Me hate-watching you during the football game caused some of it. Watching you walk toward me in gray sweats added to it. And then the nipple play was the chef's kiss on top."

I chuckled at her version of events and said, "I can't wait anymore. I want you sinking down onto my dick right now."

"Make me."

"Lift up a bit."

Bianca did as I requested, and I pulled down my boxer

briefs and sweatpants at the same time. She went back to straddling me as I grabbed the condom that I'd tossed in the cup holder earlier.

"I can't wait until I'm fucking you without this barrier," I said as I rolled the condom onto my dick.

That caused Bianca's eyes to jerk back to me. "You make it sound as if this is going to be a long-term thing."

I decided that my actions would do the talking as I grabbed her by the hips, guiding her down onto my cock.

"Oh my—" Her eyes shuttered closed, and I couldn't help but stare at the look of pure bliss on her face.

A burst of pride filled my chest because I was the one who put it there.

She moved first and I took the time to enjoy the feeling of her on me. I wished that I could flip her over and take control, but that would have to be saved for next time.

Our movements were slow at first, and the speed picked up as the need to have each other reached explosive levels. This bubble that we created was the only thing that mattered.

The only thing that would ever matter.

"I can't hold on anymore," Bianca's words came out rushed, and I was barely able to piece together what she'd said. Her nails were digging into my shoulders as she fucked me. I met her thrusts with ones of my own.

"Let go, baby," I said, and it was nothing more than a harsh whisper because I could feel my climax building. I reached up and tweaked her nipple.

That was all that was needed to start a chain reaction that ended with Bianca falling apart in my arms. Bianca cried out as she leaned forward, burying her face in the crook of my neck. The touch of her chest on mine warmed me in a way I wasn't expecting.

I continued to drive my cock into her, and I didn't stop even as she rested against me, not until I was groaning because I'd reached my climax. For a few seconds, everything went still and quiet.

As our breathing slowed down, realization about what we'd done slowly started to seep in. Had we really just fucked in the driver's seat of my SUV?

When Bianca moved her body and leaned back, I missed the feeling of her skin touching mine. She stretched her arms the best she could, and then jumped when she leaned back far enough to hit the car horn.

We stared at each other for a moment before we both started laughing uncontrollably, and any chance of the awkwardness that was bound to come after the act we'd committed, vanished into thin air.

When we finally calmed down, Bianca said, "We should probably get cleaned up and head back."

She was right, but I didn't want to. I wanted to keep her here forever, even if it didn't make a bit of sense.

I let her go and helped her back into her seat. I opened the car door to step out and grabbed my bag in order to clean up.

Once we were both dressed and sitting back in the car, I could feel Bianca staring at me. When I turned to look at her, I found her gaze slightly unsettling, as if she was searching for something in mine, but I wasn't sure what.

I started my vehicle and then asked, "Are you ready to leave?"

Bianca nodded. "I am."

With that, I put my vehicle into reverse and pulled out of the parking spot. Just like when we'd arrived, there was no one in the vicinity.

The mood on the drive back to Bianca's apartment was quiet, but content. It was a comfortable silence that I didn't mind. I couldn't stop replaying what had just happened between us, and I wondered if it would be etched into my memory for eternity.

I thought the more often I'd fucked her, the more likely I would get my fill of her and would more easily be able to push her to the side when the time came for this to end. But now, I was wondering how good of a plan this all was. The deeper into this we got, the worse I knew the outcome would be for both of us.

Bianca glanced at me, brows knitting together. "Are you okay?" she asked softly.

I forced a smile and said, "Of course. Just tired after the fun we had, not to mention the football game."

She seemed to accept my answer and dropped the subject. The rest of the ride was in complete silence, and it wasn't until I pulled up outside of her apartment building that she sighed.

Bianca reached for the door handle, but then she hesitated. "Do you want to come in?"

I wanted to, but I knew it was a bad idea. "It's getting late, and I should head back to my place."

I hated the disappointment that appeared on her face before she was able to shove it behind the mask she wore so well. "Okay. I guess I'll hear more from you about our project or about what the next provision of this deal is later."

I hate that she boiled down our time together to that, but it was understandable since that was what I had defined it as.

"That you will," I said. I moved to give her a kiss on the lips before I stopped myself. This wasn't what any of this was about, and I needed to remember that.

"Goodnight, Easton."

"Goodnight." I didn't drive away until I made sure that she was safely inside the lobby. Once she was, I drove back to my apartment, debating what the hell I was going to do next.

24

BIANCA

The following Friday as I was driving back to my apartment, my phone rang. When I saw who was calling, I sighed before I answered it.

"Hey, Mom."

"Come home for the weekend, Bianca," my mother said into the phone. "We haven't seen you in a while, and it would be nice to have you back for a bit."

I was left completely perplexed by Mom's comment. It took me a moment to come up with a response. "Why?"

"Is it weird for me to want to see my daughter every once in a while?"

I wanted to say yes, but that might lead us down a rabbit hole of an argument, and I didn't really want to go down that path. "No. Of course, I'll come home, Mom."

The cheerfulness in my voice was fake, but she didn't seem to realize it. Which was typical because she really didn't know me anyway. Although Brentson University was maybe fifteen minutes from my childhood home, I rarely, if ever, went home since starting college. Hell, I'd even taken to spending some of the vacation time we had in my apartment instead of at my parents' house.

"Excellent, do you know when I should be expecting you?"

"I can be there within the hour or so."

"Great. I'll see you then."

I hung up the phone and immediately went to pack my bookbag. Within thirty-five minutes, I was on my way to my childhood home. As soon as I turned into the long, large driveway, I was suddenly hit with memories of me driving down this road every day to go to Brentson High once I'd gotten my license.

"Home, sweet home," I whispered as I put my car into park. I looked around before I opened my door, and immediately noticed that not much had changed since the last time I'd been home, besides the weather getting cooler and the trees losing more leaves.

As I grabbed my bookbag from the passenger seat, the front door opened, and my mother stepped into the doorway.

"Glad you could make it," she said as she pulled me into a hug.

I was slightly surprised by the show of affection, but I did have to admit it felt nice to be hugged.

"Is everything okay?" I asked. I wasn't trying to be an asshole by asking, but all of this was so sudden.

"Yes, it is. I just wanted to take some time and spend it with you. Things are going to start ramping up with your father's campaign, and I wanted some time with you before things got crazy."

I was touched, yet still confused. Since when had Mom

wanted to spend time with us that didn't revolve around a photo op?

"Your father will be happy to see you," she added as she guided me into the house.

"Is he working today?" It was the weekend, but I wouldn't be surprised if he was attending an event within the community today. He had to keep up appearances of wanting to help the community he served and all of that.

"Actually, he's in his office. He's been in there all day," my mom replied.

On a Saturday? That was weird. "Has something happened?" I asked, wondering what could have been the cause.

"He told me it was just normal work stuff, so it's nothing we need to worry about. But we had to cancel our plans today because of it," she tried to reassure me.

Was that why she'd invited me over? Because Dad had canceled their plans?

"Okay, if he says so," I said, skepticism coating every word. I wasn't sure what it was about this that was giving me pause, but something was. I shook off that feeling, because I had my own shit to worry about and adding more to my plate wouldn't help matters.

"Go on up to your room and get settled. I'll start on dinner. It's a bit early, but that's fine," Mom said, leading me toward the stairs. "If Dad can join us, then he will."

"That sounds like a plan. I'll see you in a bit," I said as I made my way upstairs.

I walked into my room and placed my bookbag on the floor by my desk. I'd brought a few things I could work on while I was here anticipating my mom would likely have something come up while I was here.

My eyes landed on a picture frame I'd had on my desk and realized it was a photo of my family from about ten years ago. Mom, Dad, Nash, and me all had our arms around each other, smiling at the camera. We looked so happy in that picture, and I remember it being that way most of the time back then. That was before my father's political career had become the center of their world and was forced into mine.

With a heavy sigh, I turned away and walked down the stairs and into the foyer, which was completely empty. Before I went to find my mother, I walked toward my father's office to see if I could take a moment to say hello. My mouth dropped open due to what I heard coming from his office.

"Damn it, it's not supposed to be public knowledge!" My father's voice was filled with anger.

I couldn't help but move closer to the door because I wanted to catch every word. His office door was ajar, and through the crack, I could see him pacing back and forth with his phone pressed tightly to his ear.

"Look," he said, "if this story gets out, it'll ruin everything we've worked for. My career, my family. Everything is on the line here. Every single thing."

I could hear the strain in his voice. I needed to know what he was talking about even if my curiosity got me in trouble. This was something serious, and I needed to know what it was.

"You're supposed to keep things like this under wraps. Do your fucking job!" my father shouted.

I couldn't remember the last time I heard him swear like that. Under the anger, it was obvious that he was scared too.

"If this story doesn't disappear..." He trailed off but his threat remained.

I leaned in closer, desperate to hear more, but for the life of me, I couldn't hear who was talking to him on the other end of the phone.

"Fine." He didn't say anything else, and when I peered through the crack, the phone was no longer up to his ear. I was convinced that he'd hung up on whoever was on the other end, as all I could hear was my father's heavy breathing as he tried to rein in his emotions.

"Shit," I muttered, running a hand through my hair as I moved away from the door. Questions and concerns flew through my mind. What was that all about? It obviously was a story that involved him, and I couldn't even begin to think about what it could be referencing. What did it mean for our family if it did get out?

All I did know was, whatever my father had done, it had put our entire family at risk.

I debated telling my mother what I overheard, but then, without a doubt, she would go back to my father and tell him how she found out.

I was fucked no matter what.

For now, I had to pretend as if I'd heard nothing and as if everything was fine.

I took a deep breath, and with a final glance at my father's office door, I turned and walked down the hallway toward the kitchen. I could smell something savory coming from there, and now I was wondering if my mom was going above and beyond to put together a dinner for us.

"Hey, Mom," I said as I entered the kitchen, forcing a smile onto my face. "That smells delicious."

My mother looked up from the stove, her warm blue eyes crinkling at the corners as she smiled back at me. "I hope it tastes as good as it smells."

I sat down at the kitchen island and tried to act as if everything was normal when it wasn't. My mother was cutting up some fresh herbs, her knife rhythmically tapping against the wooden board.

"I have no doubt that it will," I said.

I suspected my mother didn't know anything about what my father was talking about on the phone. Despite all the drama between my mother and me, I felt terrible because she didn't deserve that.

"Is everything okay, Bianca?" she asked suddenly, her eyes searching mine. "You seem... distracted."

I swear my heart skipped a beat. It was the first time in a long time that I'd felt seen by her.

I shrugged. "It's been a long week."

It wasn't a lie. This had been a long enough week that I'd barely heard from Easton outside of us seeing each other while working on our psychology project.

"Alright," she said, though her eyes lingered on me for a moment longer.

I held my breath until she turned away to focus on cooking again. Some of the tension left my body knowing she wasn't going to question me right now. Questions about what I heard haunted me.

It was not only important for me to get the answers I wanted because I was curious. If this put our family's safety at stake, it was imperative that we knew as much as possible in order to react.

"Mom, do you need any help with cooking?" I offered. I needed to find a way to keep busy.

"Sure, you can finish the salad," she said, gesturing to a large bowl on the side of the sink.

I washed my hands and added the rest of the chopped veggies to the bowl. I picked up the wooden spoon next to it and began stirring the salad. But even while I focused on finishing up a part of dinner, I couldn't help but repeat everything that my father said in my head. Something bad was going to happen, and I didn't know what it was or if I could stop it.

25

EASTON

The leather couch creaked under my weight as I shifted positions again. My thoughts had taken over and were the reason I wasn't doing anything else right now.

"Damn it," I muttered under my breath as I ran a hand across my face. Thoughts of Bianca swam into my mind, and I was being driven to the brink. The way she had looked at me while we were sitting across from each other at the library or the way she looked when she was coming on my cock were all I could think about.

If it were completely up to me, I would stop hiding the connection that Bianca and I shared. I wanted to explore this freely instead of having to mostly sneak around, even though we weren't doing a great job of sneaking around if I was being honest.

I needed to talk to both Bianca and Nash. Bianca would be first, of course, because we needed to discuss whatever the fuck this was and talk about what we wanted out of it. Also, I needed to come clean about everything.

How was I going to tell Bianca the truth?

She deserved to know about the deal I struck with Nash about her. It was shitty that she didn't know now, and I wasn't sure how she would react. Nonetheless, she deserved to have the full picture, even if it meant that she'd be pissed at both me and her brother.

I was convinced she'd never forgive me.

I could picture the hurt that would cross her face when she found out. The thought killed me.

Maybe keeping this as a deal that would end when the semester did was smart.

Bianca deserved so much better than this. Better than me and what I could give her.

This whole situation was a mess, and I was trapped at its epicenter. And I couldn't blame anyone but myself.

Fuck.

My phone buzzed in my pocket, forcing me out of my thoughts. I stared down at the screen but couldn't bring myself to answer. Because it was the one person I wasn't prepared to talk to.

Nash.

I stared down at the phone, my thumb hovering over the screen. I didn't have to answer it. Ignoring it was probably my best option until I got my shit together.

The phone continued to vibrate, reminding me that I needed to make a decision about this phone call. Finally, I swiped to answer Nash and put the call on speaker.

"Hey, man," Nash said. "I wanted to talk to you about your interest in learning more about the Chevaliers. About filling you in a bit more."

That had been the last thing I'd been expecting him to

call me about, but it made sense. Mentioning anything about the secret society that he soon would be the leader of over text message would be stupid. After seeing how rough Nash looked at times, I wasn't sure this was something I wanted to do anymore, but my curiosity had been piqued.

"Easton?" Nash said when I didn't respond. "You there?"

"Yeah, sorry." My focus on Bianca had shifted to learning more about the secret society that still remained a mystery to me. "What's up?"

"I'm going to be the chairman of the Chevaliers next semester," Nash continued. "We've been watching you, Easton. We know you have what it takes to join us."

My mouth went dry because I was stunned by his admission. The Chevaliers wanted me? After trying to compete with Nash since I'd gotten to Brentson, this was the one thing that eluded me. Because of his family, he'd been an automatic shoe-in, but I hadn't been. This was the opportunity I had been waiting for. But at what cost?

"The Chevaliers are about power and prestige," Nash said slowly. "Our members hold many powerful positions all over the world, and we have influence in too many places to count. If you join us, Easton, you'll have access to opportunities you've only dreamed of."

His words resonated with me. To be able to achieve something my father hadn't been able to do would be monumental. But I was convinced there had to be a price to pay for that kind of power.

"Tell me more."

Nash went on to describe the Chevaliers vaguely. He hinted at the power and influence they wielded while revealing very little about the organization. I understood why.

I wasn't a member and wasn't allowed to know more. His words were designed to stir my curiosity but didn't satisfy me at all. I knew that was on purpose too, to make me want to join the group.

The information he was giving me was overwhelming, and each time I thought he was going to give me more, I realized he was doing nothing but causing me to think of more questions. I bit back the sigh I wanted to release as I raked a hand through my hair. Although I had time before I had to make my decision, everything suddenly felt heavy. I didn't know which option I was going to choose, not to mention, I still had Bianca to think about.

I was positive now, more than ever, that Nash had no idea about Bianca and me, because he'd be driving over here right now to fight me instead of inviting me to recruitment for the secret society he would soon be leading. Maybe we were being more careful than I thought.

"Before I let you go, tell Bianca I said hello."

Nash's words had me frozen in my tracks. Just as I thought I'd gotten out of having to speak to him about Bianca, he'd dropped that bomb on me.

"Can't you say that to her yourself? She's your sister." I spoke the words slowly and carefully, worried that this was when the explosive fight was going to occur. But it didn't make any sense given the conversation we'd just had.

"I'm just fucking with you, dude. I know that you've been hanging out because of a project for a class."

I closed my eyes and rubbed my hands across my face. Couldn't he have made a better segue into that in order to not cause me to nearly have a heart attack? "Yeah, it's been going well, even with her hating my entire existence."

"That's Bianca for you."

I didn't disagree with him because I was more than ready to get off the phone. After we said our goodbyes and I hung up, I leaned back on my couch, and found myself staring up at the ceiling. My mind was still spinning from what I'd just experienced.

Part of me was thrilled at the opportunity to potentially join the Chevaliers, the chance to be in an exclusive brotherhood with Nash. Having access to knowledge and connections beyond the ordinary student's reach would, without a doubt, be beneficial. But I also was concerned about what I might be getting myself involved in.

I closed my eyes and took time to think this over. While I mostly trusted Nash's judgment, this wasn't some small thing. If I joined the Chevaliers, there would be no going back, and I was willing to bet the only way out of the society was death.

But what should I do? That was the question of the hour.

The path ahead was dark, mysterious, and a tangled mess. I didn't know what would be standing on the other side, but what I did know was that I had some tough decisions to make.

26

UNKNOWN

I stood in the distance, watching as Bianca walked across campus. She tried to disappear in the sea of people who were also trying to get to wherever they were going, but she failed. I debated sending her another text message, but I needed to wait. It was all a part of my plan, and I needed to be careful about when I contacted her.

I was intrigued because she maintained the mask of the mayor's daughter, the façade that she'd perfected to showcase how perfect her life was even with everything falling apart. I'd only reached out to her a couple of times for now, because I didn't want to raise too much suspicion. Keeping tabs on her was just the beginning of what I'd done.

I'd been watching her brother and his girlfriend too.

But for now, my focus was on her. Only her.

I pulled my phone out of my pocket to examine the text messages I'd sent her. She'd never bothered to send one back, and she'd done her due diligence by blocking every number she'd received a text from. Not that it mattered.

Your family seems so picture perfect, but how long can you keep your family's secrets hidden?

I stuffed the phone back into my pocket and lifted the manilla envelope in my hand, it had some weight to it, and I debated with myself whether I was really going to do this.

That I was even questioning it was strange, but here we were. As I approached a USPS mailbox, I kept her in my sight until she walked into an academic building. I stuffed the envelope into the slot, and I knew what consequences it would unleash.

But I wasn't the villain.

The villain of this story could be many different things. Each and every one of them detrimental to the world the Hensons had built around them.

Good.

As I slammed the mailbox slot closed, I shrugged my shoulders and breathed a satisfied sigh.

This was all just getting started.

27

BIANCA

The warm glow from my floor lamp illuminated my apartment, but that was the only thing that felt bright in my life. Not even lighting my pumpkin-scented candles could bring me peace and shake the mood I was in.

I tucked my legs under me as I got comfortable on my couch, watching the flames of the candles burn. I hated that all my thoughts were about Easton, and how I not only wanted to have him fuck my brains out, but I wanted to spend time with him outside the bedroom too.

What had I gotten myself into?

I closed my eyes and rubbed my temples in frustration. I couldn't deny the truth any longer, and I hated it. Easton had somehow dug his way into my heart, and that scared me more than anything.

This agreement we struck was bothering me, and I knew I had to do something about it. Fast.

But what would he think and say? That was the hardest part of all of this.

"Was any of this even worth it?" I whispered to myself, groaning because I didn't have an answer to the question.

My fears about Easton and about what my father was hiding, tormented me endlessly. If I told Easton how I was feeling, and he didn't feel the same way, what would I do? If he did feel the same way I felt, would it be just as simple as us tossing our hats into the ring and seeing how a relationship between us would work? What would our families think?

There was too much to think about on top of the other priorities I was dealing with. I glared at the bottle of wine sitting on my counter, begging me to open it and just take one sip. That was all I would need to forget all this shit for a little while.

Who was I kidding? If I took one sip, it would cascade into me drinking the whole damn bottle, and then I'd be on the search for more. I needed to find something I could focus on that would take away my thoughts about Easton.

I turned on my television as a way to kill time and turn my brain off, but nothing I was even remotely interested in watching was on.

I couldn't help but remember the way that his eyes softened when he watched me, and the shift in our dynamic after we'd had sex in his SUV after his football game.

"Why is this so complicated?" I asked out loud just before I buried my face in my hands. I needed to gain enough courage to go and talk to him instead of talking to myself.

I reached over and grabbed my phone, debating whether it was a smart idea to text him to see if he was busy this evening. It was a weekday evening, so maybe he was free outside of doing homework or studying.

I stood up and stretched my body before I began my

ritual of pacing back and forth in my living room. Part of me wished that the next step I took would lead to the ground opening up and swallowing me whole. I managed to make it to my window, and I looked out at Brentson surrounding me, wondering what the hell I was going to do. I needed to decide whether I should talk to him about this or just let it go and know that he'd continue to be in my life for as long as he was in Nash's.

And then an idea popped into my head.

I spun around, and this time my walking had a purpose. I walked over to my printer and grabbed a piece of white paper. I found a pen that I hadn't put away and drew a line down the middle. On one side I wrote 'Pro' and on the other side I wrote 'Con.' This was the best way I could think of to do this without telling someone and asking for advice.

I could tell Iris about this, but I didn't want to stress her out. I was going over to her dorm in a few days anyway, to help her get ready for a ball she'd been invited to.

"Alright," I said as I tucked a strand of my blonde hair behind my ear. "Let's write these down."

I tapped my pen on my desk as my gaze slid over to the window. Then a reason came to mind.

"One pro," I said to myself. "If I talk to Easton, we can figure out what's going on between us. If we are on the same page, maybe we can... be together."

"Also," I continued, "if we discuss this, and he doesn't feel the way I do, I can move on without having the question in the back of my mind for eternity."

With a sigh, I said, "Cons... If I don't talk to Easton, I'll never know if there was anything real between us. I'll always be wondering 'what if.' Also, what if Easton rejects me? If he doesn't feel something toward me outside of fucking me, then this conversation is going to be awkward as hell, and I'll have to do my best to avoid him for until he graduated."

Which choice can I live with, and which one can I live without?

I stared at the short list before I circled one of the options and walked over to grab my phone once more. I found our texting thread from when we'd coordinated meeting up with one another, and I typed out a message before throwing myself back down on the couch.

> Me: Hey are you available tonight?

If I thought the last thirty minutes were horrible, this would be ten times worse. Now there was nothing I could do but wait.

Please answer quickly. I didn't know if I had in me to stop myself from having a panic attack because I was waiting for his response.

As if someone had heard me, my phone buzzed on the couch cushion. I took a deep breath to steady myself before I grabbed the phone and read what appeared on the screen.

> Easton: I just got out of the shower. It would be a pleasure to have you come over.

I could sense the sexual undertones in his message. Although I enjoyed it, this wasn't what I was looking for tonight.

> Me: I want to talk.

Easton: I'm down for that too.

This time I couldn't help but roll my eyes. At least his words made me smile.

Me: What time should I come over?

Easton: Whatever time works for you.

Me: How about now?

Easton: Sure.

I tucked my phone into the pocket of my jeans and grabbed my purse. I double-checked to make sure I had everything I needed in my bag before I walked out of my apartment and locked the door behind me.

Doubt crept into my mind as I drove the short distance to Easton's apartment. I was grateful that we were meeting at his place instead of him coming to mine, because I liked having an escape plan in case this didn't go the way I hoped it might go.

But will all this really be worth it? I couldn't help but think. I tried to be positive about everything, but uncertainty won out.

Once I'd parked my car and was on my way up to his apartment in the elevator, my anxiety decided to kick things up a notch. I was putting my feelings on the line and being vulnerable, with the chance of having it all smashed to pieces.

When I reached his front door, I paused as I gathered the courage to knock.

You wanted to talk to him. Now's your chance.

I needed to just do it without thinking about it any longer. I glanced to my right and then to my left before I finally knocked on the door.

"Coming!" Easton called out.

The panic within me intensified. I grabbed my phone to give my hands something to do while I waited.

And then the door opened.

I was momentarily stunned as I stared back at Easton, but thankfully, he spoke first.

"Hey, Bianca. Is everything okay?"

"I hope so. Can we talk?"

"Of course," he replied, stepping aside so that I could walk in.

I hesitated for a moment before I walked into the comfort of his home. The door clicking closed behind us screamed volumes.

"Easton," I began, my voice slightly shaky. "There's something I want to talk to you about."

"I was thinking the same thing. I also wanted to talk to you. First, would you like anything to eat or drink?"

I shook my head, but my curiosity had taken over. "You go first."

Easton seemed shocked by my suggestion. "You're my guest."

"I insist." Yes, it was me procrastinating. No, I wasn't ashamed of it.

He ran his hand through his hair, and I knew it was going to be bad.

"I wanted to talk about what happened the day after we slept together years ago."

I swallowed hard, worried about what he was going to say.

The talk I had with him that morning had been traumatic for me, so for him to bring it up, did nothing but make me more anxious.

"What did you want to say about that?"

Easton's mouth opened and closed. He looked away, one hand coming up to rub the back of his neck. "I haven't been truthful about what happened."

My gaze narrowed. "What do you mean you weren't being truthful? You told me I was just a quick fuck. We've had this conversation before."

"That wasn't everything."

I crossed my arms. "Then, please, explain."

Easton sighed and it was then I noticed he was having a hard time looking me in the eyes. This was bad. "I lied about why I pulled away. I didn't think you were a quick fuck or anything like that."

This was news to me. "So why did you pull away?"

This time, he forced himself to look me in the eye as he said, "I made a deal with your brother that I wouldn't go anywhere near you. He'd cornered me and made me promise I wouldn't mess with you the evening we met at your parents' party."

That had been the last thing I'd been thinking he would say. His confession had me in a chokehold, silencing any thoughts I wanted to say. I just stared at him in shock because there was no way that this had happened behind my back.

"Bianca, I'm so sorry."

This time, it was me fighting to open my mouth so that I could say my piece. Pain didn't begin to describe how I felt.

Rage filled me in a way I couldn't explain. "How dare the

two of you do this without my consent? I don't know who I'm pissed at more."

"Bianca, I think I can speak for both Nash and me and say neither one of us ever meant to hurt you."

"Didn't speaking for someone, aka me, get you in this situation to begin with? I would be careful about who I spoke for if I was you."

"Bianca—"

I looked away, blinking back the tears that threatened to fall. "I think I should leave." My voice came out hoarse. I stood up on shaky legs, grabbing my purse. My instincts had been right to drive myself to Easton's house because I needed to get out.

"Bianca, please don't leave like this." Easton stood too, reaching for my hand.

I jerked away from his touch.

"I'm sorry. Please give me a chance to make this right."

I shook my head, unable to form words around the lump in my throat. He'd left me mostly speechless. Without another glance at Easton, I walked out of his apartment, and I didn't bother to stick around to hear the door closing behind me with a soft click.

The cool night air did little to ease the bile that was rising from my stomach as I walked to my car. Easton's confession replayed in my mind, each word slicing into me like a chef's knife. He and my brother had made a deal about me, with no regard for how it would affect me. How could I trust anything either one of them said now?

I dug around for my keys with shaky hands. The metal bit into my palm as I gripped them tightly, using the pain to ground myself into reality.

I knew what I needed, and I needed it now.

My phone buzzed in my pocket. I pulled it out to find a text from him.

> Easton: I'm sorry for all of this, but I'm not giving up on this without a fight.

I stared at the message, anger winning the emotional war going on inside me. He had some nerve texting me right now. My fingers flew across the screen, and I pressed send before I could second guess myself.

> Me: Don't contact me again.

I turned off my phone, preventing Easton from contacting me for the time being. All of this was such bullshit.

The drive home passed in a blur. By the time I reached my apartment, exhaustion had settled into my bones. But there was something I still wanted to do, and I wouldn't be denied.

I unlocked the front door of my apartment and immediately made my way to the liquor cart. I needed to numb everything I was feeling.

With trembling hands, I grabbed a bottle of vodka and debated whether it was worth it to grab a glass. I quickly decided a glass wasn't necessary and unscrewed the top before putting the bottle up to my lips. The familiar burn of the alcohol slid down my throat, bringing with it instant relief from the pain.

Another swig of vodka went down even smoother. A warm buzz spread through my body, loosening everything.

What was I thinking? How could I have been so stupid?

I walked over to my couch and kicked off my shoes. I took another gulp of my liquor of choice and the room started to spin.

"You're fucking worthless," I yelled to no one but myself. "No one will ever want you."

I cried as my thoughts drifted to what Easton had told me. Not only did I have to deal with the betrayal from him, but from my own brother as well.

Anger took over every thought I had. I took another long pull. Darkness was starting to take control, and the alcohol was doing its best to push away everything that hurt.

I could escape from all of this. It was that easy.

When I couldn't keep a firm grip on the bottle anymore, I managed to place it on my coffee table in front of me. What I couldn't save was myself as I slowly fell off the couch and onto the floor. The world spun even more, and I wasn't sure what was up and what was down.

Was this real? Had tonight really happened?

The last thing I remembered before everything faded to black, was curling up in a ball and crying.

28

BIANCA

The soft sounds of a string quartet filtered through my home as I stood in the corner of the foyer staring at my phone. I should have been talking to our guests, but something else had drawn my attention. This time, however, it was our sound system playing the music versus my mother hiring someone.

I hated that my thoughts revolved around Easton. No matter how much I'd tried to distract myself with other things, my brain refused to completely focus on anything. I still didn't know how to feel other than angry at him and my brother. I'd been avoiding them both since I found out the truth.

I was busy waiting for Iris to contact me. Yesterday, I'd helped her get ready for a ball at the Chevalier Manor, but I hadn't heard from her since. If I didn't hear from her soon, I would drive over to Westwick to see if I could find her there.

How I managed to pull myself together to be able to go over to her dorm and help her get ready for her party after the drunken night I'd had was a miracle. It had been a difficult several days, but I managed to pull myself together enough to help her and attend this small get together at my parents' home. It was convenient that Nash wasn't here tonight, because if he was, I probably would have cursed him out.

Suddenly my phone began to vibrate and jolted me out of my thoughts. My heart began to race as I picked up the phone expecting it to be Iris. But the only thing on my screen was an unknown number. I bit my lip as I realized this was probably some kind of spam call, not Iris trying to contact me.

I looked up and the chandelier I always loved was shining bright. Too bad I didn't feel the same brightness because I was stressed about Iris and angry about Easton and Nash. Everything was fine, or so I was telling myself.

My phone vibrated again, and I wondered if someone else was calling. This time it was a text.

Unknown Number: Our game begins now.

"Bianca, I would like to talk to you in my office."

Startled, I looked up and found my father, in full Mayor Henson mode, standing in the doorway of his sanctuary with his arms crossed. I was immediately brought back to when I'd heard him yelling on the phone only a couple of weeks ago and how angry he was. Was he about to yell at me for being on my phone?

As we entered his office, the door closed with a soft thud, sealing us off from the party. My father had decided to have his office designed in shades of deep mahogany and brown and it had been like that for as long as I could remember. The big wooden desk was the focal point of the room. The bookshelf that was built into the wall contained many books and reports. While the room had overhead lights, he preferred to use a single brass lamp on his desk when it grew dark outside.

The shift in energy from the excitement out there to the frosty energy in here, was almost like whiplash. The boulder that was weighing my body down continued to get bigger. I swallowed hard as I wondered what he wanted to talk to me about.

"Sit down, Bianca," my father demanded, gesturing toward one of the leather chairs in front of his desk. Because he wasn't being more polite, I knew he was pissed. I hesitated for a moment before sinking down into the seat.

My father walked around his desk and grabbed a manila folder. He flipped the file open and pulled out several photos and laid them on the desk in front of me.

If I could have died in this chair, I would have. I immediately started to feel light-headed, I assumed as a result of the blood rapidly draining from my face.

Dad picked up one of the photos, and I immediately recognized the image. It was of me taking a shot of alcohol from Taylor's cleavage using only my mouth. The photo wasn't crystal clear, but I remembered the moment, barely. Because my face was toward her breasts and my hair had fallen into my face, it was somewhat hard to tell it was me. However, it was obvious my father had no issue identifying me.

"W-what is this? What are these?" I stuttered. There was no way I was seeing what I thought I was seeing.

"Explain this, Bianca," he said as he dropped the photos onto the desk with a flick of his wrist.

I tried to speak, but no words came out. Instead, my gaze shifted to the next photo in the row. It showed me dancing on the counter of a bar I shouldn't have even been allowed into.

"Care to tell me what's going on here?" my father continued.

Everything about him was stone cold to the point where I was very afraid.

The remaining photos were pretty bad, including one where I was sprawled across Emma's lap, my dress hiked up just a little too far. Each image was a clear reminder of the wild nights I'd spent with my friends but wasn't becoming of someone who was the daughter and of a man who had higher aspirations then his current position as Mayor of Brentson.

I was going to throw up. A million thoughts swirled in my head, including wondering how these photos had ended up in my father's possession.

And then came the real punch in my gut as I realized these were the same photos Easton had used to blackmail me into an enemies with benefits relationship with him only a few weeks ago.

That son of a bitch had no issue with betraying me again.

"There's only one way to stop this from getting out and hurting my political career and our family."

I looked up at my father, prepared to do anything to make this right. "What's that?"

"You need to marry Tristan Whitmore."

THANK YOU FOR READING! The next book in the series, Shattered Sinner, is available for pre-order now!

WANT to join the discussion about the The Brentson University Series? Click HERE to join my Reader Group on Facebook.

PLEASE JOIN my newsletter to find out the latest about The Brentson University series and my other books!

ABOUT THE AUTHOR

Bri loves a good romance, especially ones that involve a hot anti-hero. That is why she likes to turn the dial up a notch with her own writing. Her Broken Cross series is her debut dark romance series.

She spends most of her time hanging out with her family, plotting her next novel, or reading books by other romance authors.

briblackwood.com

ALSO BY BRI BLACKWOOD

Broken Cross Series

Sinners Empire (Prequel)

Savage Empire

Scarred Empire

Steel Empire

Shadow Empire

Secret Empire

Stolen Empire

The Broken Cross Series Box Set: Books 1-3

The Broken Cross Series Box Set: Books 4-6

The Ruthless Billionaire Trilogy

The Billionaire's Auction

The Billionaire's Possession

The Billionaire's Vengeance

Brentson University Series

Devious Game

Devious Secret

Devious Heir

The Westwick University Duet

The Lies Beneath

The Truth Between

The Shattered Trilogy

Shattered Saint

Shattered Sinner

Shattered Reign

www.ingramcontent.com/pod-product-compliance
Lightning Source LLC
Chambersburg PA
CBHW061542210726
48287CB00006B/2054